Grange

A Grange Hill schoo[...] [gov]ernors, it all sounded v[...] Michael Doyle as he [...] [out]side the staff-room door. What goes on at school camps is nobody's business; people get up to all sorts of tricks, think nobody's looking. Then the staff go back and give a nice report to the headmaster and parents. But suppose somebody came back with another kind of report – like the truth – like what they *really* get up to. How? His new camera would be just the job. It's got the lot, telescopic lens, develops its own pictures ...

But even Doyle's vivid imagination fell short of the truth, and he'd reckoned without the intervention of a very determined Penny Lewis and a very obstinate Tucker Jenkins and friends, who seemed set to thwart his plans.

ROBERT LEESON

# Grange Hill Goes Wild

Based on the BBC television series
GRANGE HILL
By Phil Redmond

FONTANA · LIONS

First published in Fontana Lions 1980
by William Collins Sons & Co Ltd
14 St James's Place, London SW1

Printed in Great Britain
by William Collins Sons & Co Ltd, Glasgow

# Chapter 1

Early Friday evening at Grange Hill, near the end of term on a typical English summer day. All is quiet. The only sound is the rain drumming on the top of the covered ways and the pattering feet of half-starved mice retreating from the school cafeteria. Everyone has gone home, even Tucker Jenkins and Benny Green who have been in detention. The school seems to be empty.

No. A lone figure is loitering in the corridor near the Head's office. Michael Doyle is hanging about waiting for a lift home. His father, Councillor Doyle, chairman of governors no less, is in with the Head, discussing the School Fund.

Michael, bless his warm heart, is hoping for more than a lift home. He's hoping for a few snippets of information for that active brain of his to get to work on. Michael Doyle's brain is not widely appreciated in Grange Hill, which is a pity. Because Michael had plans for the school, or rather for some of the people in it – like boiling them in oil, or feeding them gently through the waste disposal unit.

He had a list, not on paper, Michael is far too intelligent for that, but in his mind. It included all the people who had annoyed him, or got in his way, or interfered with his perfectly reasonable plans to be Ruler of the Universe. To be quite honest, it was a revenge list, a hit list.

Top of the list came Jenkins and his sidekicks for crimes too numerous to mention. Then Penny Lewis, crusading journalist of the year who brought Doyle's promising career as a school politician to a grinding halt. Trisha Yates, who had nearly poisoned him during that moronic semolina business. And staff, too – Hopwood, a real do-gooder. And Peterson. No woman had a right to push Michael Doyle around.

As he paced quietly up and down, Michael had one of

those brainwaves, those strokes of genius which marked him out from lesser folk.

In a flash he saw where he had gone wrong so far. He had tried to pick them off one by one, when he should have been working out the master plan to sink them all without trace. He had been messing about with tactics when he should have gone in for grand strategy.

His aimless walking had brought him to the passage outside the staff room. He stopped in surprise. He heard voices. For he was standing underneath the ventilator. And as Michael alone knew, anyone who leaned quietly against the wall at this point could hear everything that went on inside. He listened now and after a while realized that he had tuned in to a meeting. There was Baxter's voice, loud and hearty, Hopwood's quieter tones, Miss Peterson and Mrs Thomas from biology. At first he had difficulty in telling what they were saying. They all seemed to be talking at once, in excited tones. Gradually Doyle realized this was a crisis meeting. There was trouble in the air.

Pressing himself closer to the wall he began to make out what they were talking about. Could it be? Yes, it could – it could be just what Dr Doyle ordered – the kind of situation where he could stir to his heart's content. Yes indeed, they could look out, now, the lot of them.

# Chapter 2

Inside the staffroom, Mr Baxter, known as Bullet, stood legs astride, hands on hips, looking down at his colleagues who were stretched out in battered armchairs. Mr Hopwood held a small notebook to his chest, Mrs Thomas sat with eyes closed as if the week had been too much for her. Miss Peterson eyed Baxter, her eyebrows slightly raised.

'The question is,' said Baxter, 'do we cancel the school holiday or don't we?'

'The question is, Geoff dear,' said Miss Peterson, 'do you always have to loom over us like that. It's not the kids you're intimidating now, you know.'

'Ha,' snorted Baxter, 'the day someone intimidates you, we'll run the flag up.' Miss Peterson smiled without replying and Baxter sat down in a chair which twanged quietly in protest.

'Well, do we or don't we?' he demanded. 'We started off with two hundred and a fortnight at Butlin's. Now we're down to fifty kids, five staff, a dozen tents and a patch of grass in the back of beyond.'

He glared at Hopwood's grinning face.

'What's so funny?'

Hopwood looked serious. 'Just the way you put it, that's all. But it's either that or nothing. And if Mrs Thomas's cousin hadn't happened to know this farmer we wouldn't even have the patch of grass, not at this time in the summer.'

Mrs Thomas opened her eyes.

'That's the size of it. When they took the subsidy away, that put paid to the holiday camp. Then the governors queried all that money spent last year buying camping equipment for the outdoor centre ...'

'Huh,' said Baxter, 'all what money? Enough tents for about fifty? How they expect us to do anything these days beats me. They soon complain if we don't get results, though.'

Hopwood nodded. 'Yes, and it'll get worse. Of course we could just pack it in, tell the parents the school trip's axed. We'd be perfectly justified.'

Miss Peterson shook her head. 'And kids like Benny Green and Richard Marks and quite a few others get no holiday away. School meals, school books, where are they going to stop?'

Mrs Thomas cleared her throat. 'I absolutely agree with you, but at the risk of being a bore I have to remind you, this ain't a union meeting. It's an emergency meeting about a school camp.'

'Right.' Baxter sat up. 'Tell us a bit more about this place Dan,' he said to Hopwood.

Hopwood eased himself up in his chair. 'Nice place, really. Half way up a river valley, with some thick old woods, part of a neglected estate, bit of easy moorland. Next to an old wartime airfield, bit isolated ...'

'How isolated?'

'Three miles from the village. But that could be convenient – keep the kids from wandering off too much.'

'Blow the kids,' muttered Baxter. 'I'm thinking of us and the pub at nights.'

'There's the minibus, and of course there's one bus to and fro every evening.'

'And what will we offer the clients?'

Hopwood smiled. 'Oh, that's not bad. Downstream there's canoeing and upstream, in the hilly part, there's pony trekking. We can have nature trails, there's loads of room for rounders, cricket, football.'

'Swimming?' asked Miss Peterson.

'Not sure about that, unless we can improvise something.' Hopwood looked out of the window. 'Still, in this weather maybe they won't want to.'

Mrs Thomas sighed. 'Don't say that. The weather must improve.'

She went on curiously: 'What's the field like?'

'Slopes a bit ...'

'Thought so – they always do.'

Hopwood went on. 'Slopes nicely down to the stream. There's an old oak tree in the middle. There's a hut, like an ex-army place with room for mess tables and a field kitchen. The farmer's laid on water there and there are more taps and stone tops for washing further up the field.'

'Minimum facilities, as they say,' grunted Baxter. 'OK, OK. So we can make a camp out of that. But what about policing it? Five of us for fifty of them won't do.'

'Who's the five?' asked Mrs Thomas.

'The four of us, plus Roy Wilmot. He's not staff officially and he's finished his teaching practice, but he's volunteered to come along.'

'Good old Roy. He's a real boy scout. He might even make a good teacher one day,' said Miss Peterson.

'Hm, maybe,' returned Baxter. 'Right now he's too innocent. Still believes pupils are human.'

'Roy's not *so* innocent,' countered Hopwood. 'I think he wants to include the school camp in some kind of project he's doing for a degree ...'

'Ah, nature in the raw ...'

'We're drifting from the point,' said Miss Peterson. 'How come we only have five? What about Graham Sutcliffe and Terri Mooney?'

'Hadn't you heard? Graham's pulled out. Say's he's finished with being the school's dogsbody. Being lumbered with the tuck shop finished him off. And that, of course, means we don't get Terri either ...'

'That's jumping to conclusions,' interrupted Miss Peterson.

Baxter went on. 'On the other hand, we might be better off without Miss Mooney ...'

'Now look,' interrupted Miss Peterson, 'I know Terri's absent minded, but ...'

'Absent minded?' retorted Baxter. 'That's the understatement of the year.'

Hopwood looked embarrassed. 'There'll be three sixth

formers. They're always a big help.'

'Aha, who?'

'Dukeson for one, and Gary Hargreaves.'

'Good, they're real troupers. Who else?'

'Eddie Carver.'

'What does he want with the school camp? He's supposed to have left school.'

'Well, he's volunteered. And he's very handy with tents and camping gear.'

'Yes, and very nippy with pints of scrumpy and a quick how's your father in the shrubbery.'

'Don't give a dog a bad name, Baxter.'

Baxter bellowed with laughter. 'I didn't give Carver a bad name. He's worked on it for the past two years. If old age hadn't caught up with him, we'd have had to show him the door.'

Mrs Thomas held her hand up. 'Beggars can't be choosers. If Eddie Carver wants to help, I shan't say no. But that doesn't solve the real problem. We have twenty-four boys, twenty-two girls and only two female staff.'

The others fell silent. Hopwood pulled himself up from the chair and headed for the sink and the tea things. Baxter looked gloomily out of the window which was streaming with rain. The silence deepened.

Suddenly there was a commotion in the corridor. A woman's voice was heard, high pitched but commanding.

'Michael Doyle, will you clear off home! What's that? Your father? I don't care if he's interviewing the Pope. Clear off home.'

Inside the staffroom eyebrows were raised, glances exchanged. The door burst open and Terri Mooney, face flushed, eyes sparkling, hair towsled, charged in.

'Sorry I'm late. Have you finished the discussion about the camp?'

'Well, no,' said Baxter awkwardly. 'We thought you weren't coming –'

'Why not?'

'Well, Graham said ...'

10

Miss Mooney's face went crimson. 'I don't live in Graham's pocket you know. I'm coming to the camp.'

'Oh, that's splendid.' Baxter turned to the others. 'There we are – what did I say?'

Miss Peterson choked. Mrs Thomas looked at the ceiling Mr Hopwood said hastily.

'You're just in time for a cup of tea, Terri.'

# Chapter 3

Michael Doyle was so shocked at Miss Mooney's outburst that he took off along the corridor and was at the school entrance before he remembered he was supposed to be getting a lift home from his father. But by that time his mind was in full gear working on what he had just heard.

School camp. Aggro with the governors. It all sounded promising. Now where could he fit in? To be honest he hadn't planned to go on the school trip anyway. And certainly not now it was to be camping out. That was strictly for scouts and guides and people who'd never had the benefits of civilization. Normally a tent was the last place he would spend a holiday. On the other hand, all kinds of things went on in school camps.

He abondoned the idea of waiting for his Dad, and leaving the school at the double, he raced through the rain across the main road to the shopping centre. Picking the one phone box which was working he quickly dialled the number for his mate Macker's home. After a few seconds Macker himself answered.

'Hey, come down the caff in the Arndale.' It wasn't an invitation. Doyle expected his men to move when he gave the word.

'I'm watching something on the box,' protested Macker.

'Don't you know it rots the mind? That's a joke in your case. You get down here double quick. And pick up Robo on the way.'

Doyle put the phone down, left the kiosk and wandered into the caff. It was half empty now and most of the tables had chairs on top. He took a quick look round. One or two kids were there, but no Grange Hillites. He did not want them around when he was discussing business. He bought himself a cup of coffee and settled down.

Ten minutes later, Macker and Robo strolled in. They hesitated a minute, then saw that Doyle was not treating them this time and reluctantly got their own coffee. Doyle let them sit down.

Then briefly and simply he put his plan to them. The three of them would sign on for the school camp, like good boys, take part in all the activities.

Macker and Robo looked at him in disbelief.

'Go camping? You're off your runners,' said Macker, shaking his head pityingly.

'Listen, clay brain,' said Doyle. 'You know what goes on at school camps. People do all sorts of things they shouldn't, things parents don't know about. And teachers get up to all sorts of malarkey because they think nobody's looking. Then they come back and give a nice report to the governors and the parents' meeting and everybody pats them all on the head and says, "isn't it marvellous".'

'So?'

'So, suppose someone came back with another kind of report – like the truth – like what they really get up to? What all these lovely teachers do on their free holiday.'

'Free?'

'Course it is. They get so many free fares from British Rail, then there's money from the School Fund. They put themselves down on expenses, get it? And nobody asks what they really get up to ...'

'I've heard some dodgy things about school trips,' said Robo, waking up suddenly.

'Well, this time there's going to be a full report. With illustrations,' said Doyle.

'With what?'

'My new camera, that's what. It's got the lot, telescopic lens, develops its own ...'

To Doyle's surprise, Macker showed no enthusiasm.

'Get off,' he said. 'They'll sus you out in ten minutes, poking that camera in around the bushes.'

'Not if there's someone around to distract attention.'

'Like who?'

13

'Like *you*, dummer,' Doyle was beginning to get annoyed. He wan't used to questions like this.

Macker stood up and kicked his chair back.

'Well you can get lost, Mickey. I'm not sleeping in a sodding tent and risking getting a kicking from somebody – that's what I'd do to a Peeping Tom, anyway.'

'Hey, watch it,' said Doyle, as he saw Robo grinning.

Macker bent over the table. 'You watch it mate. I'm taking it easy these holidays. The last caper you got up to we ended up sorting through the school dustbins looking for Penny Whatsit's project folder with Jenkins and his mob laughing their socks off.'

'Dah, it won't be like that ...'

'No? It'll be worse.' Macker raised his voice so that the woman behind the counter looked inquisitively at them.

'I'm not going up the jungle for you or anybody else. So stuff it.'

With that, he walked out, jerking his head at Robo who slowly, with one eye on Doyle, slid out after him.

Doyle watched them go. He didn't say a word. For once words failed him. He bit his lip. Then he got up and ordered himself another coffee. This needed thinking out again. He was set on his scheme. But without a bodyguard he'd have to go very, very carefully. Drinking his second cup, he brooded over the whole business. Maybe a one-man operation would be better. When all was said and done, Macker and Robo could be real thickoes at times.

He got to his feet to leave. But the woman at the counter called him back. Macker and Robo hadn't paid.

# Chapter 4

Back in the staff room the atmosphere was more cheerful. The five teachers had been joined by the student Roy, tall, thin, fair-haired, with baby-blue eyes and an eager manner. Over the second pot of tea, they had got down to checking the lists of pupils who had paid for the camp.

Baxter supped his tea with relish and asked:

'How many does that make, Roy old son?'

Roy ran his pencil down the list and muttered to himself. 'Thirty-nine, I think,' he said at last, 'or maybe forty.'

'Who else have we got then?'

Mrs Thomas held up a scrap of paper.

'Duane Orpington.'

Miss Peterson's eyebrows rose.

'I'm surprised his father'd pay for it.'

Mrs Thomas nodded. 'Tell you the truth, I think our Duane's saved the money himself. He's very keen.'

'Probably anything to get out of reach of his old man,' said Hopwood. 'Still, he won't have his little friend Tracy with him will he?'

'Why not?'

'Flown away. Her Dad's taken the whole family off. No work down here.'

'Karen Stanton's missing too. I thought she'd be on the list, but no. Looks as though things at home aren't too good.'

'Hm, who have we got, then?' said Baxter impatiently.

'There's Patterson – the plump one. Very handy with tents and such like.'

'What he needs is a slimming course. We'll ration his mashed spud and tinned pud.'

'Same goes for Anita Unsworth.'

'She can't be coming! She hates fresh air.'

15

'Ah, but her Gran says it's good for her, so Anita's coming.'

'Who else?'

'Christopher Stewart.'

'He'll stand some watching – proper little Red Robbo, he is.'

'Oh, come on. He's a bright lad. Just knows his rights, that's all.'

'So do we all. Who's next?'

'Precious Matthews.'

'Who?'

'West Indian girl – tall, handsome.'

'Hm, I know her. That is one stroppy young lady ...'

Baxter caught Miss Peterson's glance and put his hand up in mock alarm.

'I know, Maureen, I know what you're going to say. She's black and female, so she has a lot to put up with.'

'No,' glared Miss Peterson. 'She just won't be pushed around, that's all.'

'Do let's get on,' said Mrs Thomas. 'It's nearly six o'clock. I've a home to go to if you people haven't.'

Hopwood picked up his notebook and read.

'Pamela Cartwright.'

'Don't know her ...'

'Short-haired, sporty. She'll be very handy on the pony trekking.'

'Good. Who else?'

'Trisha Yates.'

'And Cathy Hargreaves, I suppose.'

'No, Cathy's staying at home this time. Mum's not well and with Gary at the camp, she wants one of them with her.'

'Justin Bennett?'

'No, not Justin. With Andrew Stanton staying away, Justin's giving it a miss. There's Alan Humphreys ...'

'And Susi MacMahon, I suppose.'

'Yes.'

'Hey, with Alan, Susi and that sixth former Carver we could run a judo course, perhaps.'

Miss Peterson made a face. 'I'm not sure Alan cares very much for Eddie Carver.'

'Why so?'

'Can't you guess? Little too much attention to Susi.'

'Right,' said Baxter, 'let's speed this up. Who else?'

Hopwood looked slyly at him.

'Benny Green ...'

'Yes?'

'And the one I've saved for last, Peter Jenkins.'

Baxter shot upright in his chair.

'I'm not having him.'

'He's coming, like it or not. His parents are off to Spain for those two weeks and Peter is coming camping. You have to put up with it.'

Baxter's face creased in gloom. 'If you say so, but I'm sure we'll regret it.'

Miss Peterson grinned. 'Bet you won't.'

Baxter stood up. 'How much?'

'Fiver,' she said boldly.

'Not enough. Tenner at least.'

'I'll have a fiver on Peter,' said Hopwood. 'I think he'll turn out for the best and you won't regret it.'

'Ha ha,' shouted Baxter. 'Done. For a tenner, Jenkins can come.'

# Chapter 5

While the teachers at Grange Hill were putting their money on Tucker Jenkins, he had other things on his mind. To be precise, he had no intention of going to the camp. Michael Doyle had that very evening tried to persuade his mates to come to the camp. But Tucker was bent on doing exactly the opposite.

He stood with Alan Humphreys and little Benny Green sheltering from the rain by the wall of the garages behind the flats where he lived, the grey sky growing more grey as the evening wore on. In fact, with the weather and the prospect of spending two whole weeks under damp canvas, far from the high street and the chippy and all that made life worth while, Tucker might have been very depressed. But in fact, being Tucker, he had already thought of a way out. He had a plan and was now doing his best to sell it to two very unwilling buyers.

'See, we don't have to go.'

'But I want to,' said Benny Green.

'No you don't. You don't know your own mind. It's just your Mum's put the idea into your head. Now repeat after me, "I do not want to go to the school camp." You'll feel better then.'

'Anyway, I want to go,' said Alan, suddenly looming over Tucker.

'Hey, calm down,' said Tucker. 'You just want to go because you think you're going to ride off into the wet sunset with Susi don't you . . .'

'Get off,' said Alan, but he looked faintly embarrassed.

'Well, I've got news for you, Humphreys old soul. When Eddie Carver gets going, Susi's going to leave you gasping.'

'You're out of your tiny one,' said Alan. But Tucker shook his head, irritatingly. 'I have inside information that

18

you are wasting your time and Miss MacMahon is now going for the more mature, slimmer, cigar-smoking man.

'What's more, Eddie Carver, who happens to be a forearm man of the ninety-third dan, is just waiting for the chance to fasten your shoes round your neck, with your feet still in 'em.'

Seeing Alan's face, Benny intervened hastily.

'Anyway, Tucker, what is all this. You're going to the camp anyway. So why not just go with it?'

Tucker shook his head. 'I am not going to the camp.'

'But what'll your Dad say? He'll murder you if you don't go.'

'He won't know, see. They'll be in Spain, won't they?'

'Yes, sure, but I know your Dad. He'll make sure you're down at the station and on the train before they go to the airport.'

Tucker grinned knowingly. 'Yeah, but if we ask Alan's dad to run us to the station in his van, he never hangs about does he? So when he's gone, we wait quietly around until the camping mob are on the train, then we do a bunk. Bullet thinks we've just not turned up and shares out the rations with the others. Easy!'

Benny shook his head in puzzlement.

'But what do we do then? I can't go back home, me Dad'll skin me. And if you go back to your place, it'll be all round the block in no time and your Dad'll just vaporise you when he gets back.'

Tucker looked up at the sky. The rain had stopped and the clouds had begun to lift.

'Follow me, men,' he said, with a wave of his hand and set off at a good pace, followed reluctantly by his mates. Instead of aiming for the high road, he strode along Kettlewell Street and then, making a sharp right turn, led them up the hill into streets where the houses were older and bigger with larger gardens.

In a small side road he halted them in front of a row of three-storey terraced houses with empty windows and frontages covered in scaffolding. In the gardens lay heaps of bricks, and a huge skip half full of rubbish stood by the pavement. He pointed to a top floor window.

'There you are.'

'What's that?' asked Alan staring at Tucker.

'That's a squat.'

'A squat?' said Benny. 'I thought squats were for homeless people.'

Tucker grinned. 'If we don't go to the camp, we'll be homeless, won't we.'

'What, live there for two weeks? On bare boards?'

Tucker shook his head. 'Three bedrooms with matresses. Our kid and his mates are doing a conversion job on this place. They use it with their girl friends now and then. It's even got a phone in – they never knocked it off.'

Alan said nothing but stared moodily up at the house. Benny's mind was already ticking over.

'All right, but what do we live off?'

'We've got our pocket money, right? Then we rent out rooms.'

'We what?'

'Like our kid does. We charge a oner a night for blokes who want to stay out late. They say they're staying with a mate's family. They even give their parents a phone number. Then maybe once or twice we let the place out for a party. Listen, we could even be in pocket at the end of a fortnight. We sleep in comfort, eat well – no wet blankets, no earwigs, no Smash and beans, no Baxter PT sessions, no seeing Pongo Yates in her nightie every morning.'

At last, to his relief, he saw a grin spread over Benny's face.

'OK, you're on,' he said. But Alan frowned.

'I think it's stupid.'

'Please yourself,' said Tucker, pleasantly. 'All you've got to do is organize your Dad as chauffeur and keep your mouth shut. But, you know, you're going to change your mind.'

# Chapter 6

Yet another member of the camping party was making plans that Mr Baxter and his general staff had no idea of. He made his plans in silence and alone, because they were much more serious.

Duane Orpington had planned to go to the camp from the start. He'd saved all the money he could and even sold his bike for five quid to a bloke in his year at school, promising delivery on the day he returned from his trip. He hadn't told his Dad about that – too right he hadn't told his Dad. But not telling his Dad had become quite an art with Duane.

If he told his Dad anything he got thumped for sure. If he didn't tell him anything, and his Dad found out, he got thumped worse. But sometimes he didn't find out. And Duane was getting better and better at making sure his Dad didn't find out. He'd long ago given up expecting his Dad to play fair in this game, so *he'd* stopped playing fair. And this time he was going to play the game right through according to his own rules.

He was bunking off – for real – for good. He wasn't coming back. And he was using the trip to camp to make sure he had a head start. He knew what would happen if he tried it, made a mess of it and then had to go back home.

His plan was only half worked out. It all hung on one thing. This place they were going to, the camp ground. It was right next door to an airfield. He'd seen it on the sketch map Mrs Thomas had given him. It wasn't a big airfield, not like London Airport or Gatwick or wherever, but it would have planes going a fair way. Planes would load up on the runways. And somebody as small as he was, and as quick, could slide up through the loading hatch just as they finished stowing cargo away.

He didn't try to work out his plan in too much detail. It

was simple, so it was good. He'd take it a stage at a time. He might need two or three goes at it. But he'd do it. And he wouldn't tell anyone. This kind of plan was best done on your own.

If Tracy had still been around, would he have told her? He didn't know. But Tracy wasn't around. Her Dad had taken off looking for work up in Scotland and just dragged the whole family away with him. Fathers did what they liked, just when it suited them. Well, it didn't suit him any more.

In the quiet of his own bedroom, Duane took out his rucksack and very carefully began to pack it, checking his clothes, his gear and his money for the last time.

This journey was for real.

# Chapter 7

*CAMP LOG: Day One*: ETD 0830 hours from Paddington Station. Our party, fifty pupils and six staff (including Mr Wilmot, student teacher), had a reserved carriage to Welbourne Junction – approximate journey five hours (packed lunch on train). At Welbourne Junction we caught the local diesel train, packing it out to the dismay of some of the local people, to Fawley Grange. From Fawley village we were ferried in the school mini-bus, taken down earlier by Mr Hopwood and the sixth-formers, three miles to the camp site. It took five journeys and even then we were breaking regulations according to Mr Baxter. Everyone hungry and exhausted when we began to set up camp at 1700 hours under low, grey skies. Fortunately no rain as yet..

Fairly uneventful journey. Except that our party has four missing – three at the beginning of the trip, one at the end.

(Signed – PENNY LEWIS)

# Chapter 8

Tucker's plan worked like a dream – as far as it went.

Alan Humphreys' Dad, as agreed, ferried the three of them down to Paddington. And as predicted, he chatted for two or three minutes, then waved goodbye and took off at high speed. Meanwhile, as planned, Mr and Mrs Jenkins were safely on their way to the airport, and Mr and Mrs Green had left by easy stages to have a day out at Southend.

As planned, Mr Humphreys had brought Tucker, Benny and Alan down to the station in good time. Platform 5 approach was empty of Grange Hillites. Tucker and Benny, with Alan reluctantly helping, shifted their gear and stowed it behind a block of telephone kiosks from where they could keep the platform under observation without being seen. They settled down with cans of coke and waited.

Five minutes later people began to roll up – Bullet Baxter, Miss Peterson.

'Hey, Baxter's in shorts,' chuckled Benny.

'Rather see Peterson in shorts,' answered Tucker.

'Shut up,' snapped Alan.

'Hey, what's up with you? Oh-Oh, look,' Tucker nudged Benny, who peered out from behind their hideout.

A taxi had pulled up at the approach and out of it, humping their gear, tumbled three sixth formers – Dukeson, Gary Hargreaves, Eddie Carver and behind them Susi MacMahon. She refused Carver's offer to carry her rucksack, but didn't seem to mind as he strolled her up to the barrier with his arm round her shoulder.

'What'd I tell you?' whispered Tucker.

'Shut up or I'll shut you up,' threatened Alan. Tucker shut up. He knew when Alan was serious and what he would do about it.

Pongo Yates rolled up, with sister Carol to see her off. There was Penny Lewis, being seen off by her fussy mother and trying to get rid of her quickly. A whole crowd of parents arrived bringing first and second years, all dumping their gear at the barrier. The crowd grew thicker. All the staff had arrived. Now Baxter was doing a head count.

'He can't balance the books,' muttered Tucker in Benny's ear.

'Hey, lay off, will you,' said Benny as Tucker's weight nearly sent him sprawling.

'Look. They're going to start searching now,' said Alan anxiously.

'Get off,' said Tucker, 'don't talk wet.'

But Alan was right. Baxter and Miss Peterson were beginning to pace up and down the station approach, looking at their watches. Now Mrs Thomas joined in and began to range the barrier, coming dangerously close to where they were hiding.

'Let's pull out,' said Benny.

'Where to?'

'Back behind the bookstall.'

'What about the gear?'

'Leave it there. Even if they see it, they won't know whose it is. Tell you what, pull it in a bit.'

'Hey, no.'

Now Mrs Thomas was there on the other side of the phone booth. But at the last moment she stopped and turned her back. The three retreated, leaving their gear in disorder, one rucksack sticking out from behind the booth.

In the shadow of the bookstall they looked back.

Tucker elbowed Alan.

'Hey, they're giving up. They're going.'

Sure enough, Bullet was waving the whole crew through the barrier.

Now the platform approach was clear.

'Come on,' urged Tucker. 'Let's get the gear and clear out.'

They tumbled back to the phone booth. But Tucker stopped short so that Alan ran into the back of him and knocked him flying. Picking himself up, Tucker looked wildly round.

'What's up?' said Benny. 'Stop messing about, Tucker.'

My rucksack, bird-brain, that's what.'

'What about it?'

'It's gone.' Sure enough, only two rucksacks were left.

Tucker went pale: 'Someone's nicked it.'

'Can't have. We were only gone two secs,' said Alan. 'Let's have a look round. Come on, Benny. You stay here and watch the other gear, Tucker.'

Two seconds later, Tucker heard a great shout from the barrier. He looked across to see Alan waving and pointing down the platform.

'Look, a bloke's got it.'

Tucker leapt to his feet, grabbed both bags and staggered to the barrier. Alan and Benny took them from him and the three burst through the gate just as the ticket collector tried to shut it. Ahead of them, they saw a tall, fair haired young man, carrying Tucker's rucksack by the straps, climbing on to the train.

'Hey,' yelled Tucker. 'Stop him.'

At the shout, the guard further down the platform, who had his flag raised, dropped his arm. Tucker, Benny and Alan, panting like out of condition greyhounds, reached the train just as the young man hauled himself aboard. Tucker flung himself up the steps.

'Excuse me sir, but you've taken my bag by mistake.'

The young man turned, mouth wide in astonishment.

'Oh, but I thought it belonged to the Grange Hill Party.'

'No, sir,' lied Tucker desperately. 'Can you pass it to us, please.'

He stepped forward. Bewildered, the young man picked up the rucksack and held it out.

Just then came the shriek of a whistle. A great jerk from the carriage. The train was moving.

'Oh no,' groaned Tucker as he grabbed his rucksack and

struggled back to the door. What had happened to his plan? He was being whipped off to the camp, and Alan and Benny were being left behind.

# Chapter 9

Just as suddenly, the whole train shuddered to a halt, shooting the young man on top of Tucker and sliding the two of them down towards the door. Thankfully, Tucker, scrambled to his feet, picked up his rucksack and reached for the door handle. But even as he did so, the door was plucked violently open, two bodies complete with rucksacks were hurled into the corridor sending Tucker to the floor for a second time.

Before he could disentangle himself, there was another huge wrench, a groan from the train and the whole lot was in motion again.

Tucker sat on the corridor floor looking at Alan and Benny stretched out across one another.

'Pin-brains. What'd you get on for? I had it made.'

Alan glared at him: 'How did we know? We thought the flipping train was going with you in it.'

The three of them clambered to their feet and came face to face with the baffled blue eyes of the young man who had taken Tucker's gear. He stared at them.

'You know, I could have sworn you three were with the Grange Hill Fawley Grange camping party.'

'Oh no, sir,' said Tucker, driving a neat elbow into Alan's ribs before he could open his mouth. 'It's all a big mistake.'

'Well, I'm sorry. But you see, we were three boys missing – Jenkins, Humphreys and Green. I was sure they were you – I mean you were they.'

'Oh no, sir – I mean – we've heard of them, but ...'

'You've heard of them. But ...?'

Tucker had an inspiration. 'You see sir, we're from Brookdale. We're supposed to be on a hiking trip to – er Penzance.'

28

The young man's face brightened. 'Well that's not so serious then. You can change at Swindon and get another train. Anyway,' he grinned. 'Why don't you come and join us in our compartment. We do have three empty places and the train's crowded.'

He pointed along the train. 'It's two or three carriages down.'

Tucker shook his head.

'Well no, sir. You see, sir, it might not be a good idea for us to join you. You see there's been a lot of aggro, I mean bother, between Grange Hill and Brookdale in the past. There might be bad feeling. I mean some of your people know us very well.'

'Just as you like.' The young man turned to go.

'Sir,' called Tucker, 'you won't mention to anybody will you. I mean there could be trouble. I mean it could lead to the train being wrecked.'

When the young man had gone, Alan turned on Tucker.

'You are out of your tiny bonce,' he said furiously. 'All that garbage about being Brookies.'

'Ah, calm down,' said Tucker. 'I straightened it out didn't I? All we've got to do now is bed down and wait for Swindon. Then we get the next train back.'

'Yeah? And what do we do for tickets?'

'Dead easy. Every time the ticket collector comes we slip into the toilets.'

'Well, start practising now,' said Benny, suddenly. 'Because someone's coming.'

They piled into the nearest toilet. It was agony, British Rail toilets are a tight fit for one, let alone three, with one built like Humphreys. 'It's killing me,' gasped Benny, 'that handle's sticking in me ...'

'Shut up,' said Tucker. 'I'll open the door a bit.'

He pulled back the door an inch or two and looked out.

'Hey,' he whispered, 'look who's here.'

'Who cares?' grunted Alan, 'All I can see is the back of Benny's ...'

29

'Look. It's Doyley out there hiding in a corner. He's up to something.'

Sure enough, in the corner, between luggage rack and door, Doyle was crouching over something. Tucker, to muffled groans from Benny and Alan, forced the door further open. Doyle was fiddling with a camera – and a real beauty too. If Tucker had one like that he'd be showing it off to everybody. What was Doyley up to, the oily rat?

'For crying out loud, Tucker. Let's get out of here.'

At the sound of Alan's voice Doyle looked up. Quick as lightning he focused his camera on the door opening. Tucker could move smartly to, With a great heave which almost ruined Alan's prospects for ever, he forced the door open and jumped at Doyle, snatching the camera from him. Stepping sideways, he used his other hand to push down the window.

'Right, Oily. What are you up to, or this goes out of the train.'

'You're crazy, Jenkins. What are you all hiding in the toilet for? You're supposed to be going to camp.'

'Yeah, and what're you messing about with that camera for, taking snaps of people in the bogs? That's bent!'

'Don't be stupid. There isn't a film in it. I was just going to put one in when you jumped me,' said Doyle. He watched in pain as Tucker held the camera up to Benny and Alan who had now crawled from their cramped hiding place. Alan took the camera and fiddled with the back. It sprang open. He shook his head.

'No film there. So give it back to him Tucker. If you damage that it's two ton up your jumper.'

Tucker shrugged. 'OK. Now look Doyle. Just go back where you came from. You haven't seen us. We haven't seen you. Right. I don't know what you're up to, but as long as you leave us out of it, OK. Right?'

Doyle took back his camera gratefully and sidled away along the train.

'Right now, subjects,' said Tucker. 'Make yourselves comfortable. Get ready to bail out at Swindon.'

But someone had given someone a bit of duff information. The train didn't stop at Swindon. It sailed right through and on to Welbourne Junction. Every turn of the wheel brought Tucker closer to camp.

# Chapter 10

The train was held up in the sticks west of Swindon, and by the time it reached Welbourne Junction, around three in the afternoon, Benny and Alan were ready to give in. They'd finished Alan's sandwiches and Benny's orange squash that his mother had made up, and were ready to start on Tucker's rucksack. But like a wise general he held them back. His bag was for emergency rations, he told them. And like a good general, he rallied his troops at the darkest hour.

'It'll be dead easy. All we have to do at the Junction is keep out of sight. Then nip over to the other platform and get the next train up to town.'

And thanks to Tucker's brilliant tactics, it *was* dead easy. As the train slowed down for the junction he led them, baggage and all, right to the rear of the train. As the train stopped, at Tucker's command, the three of them bailed out and hid behind an old shack at the end of the platform. Out of sight, perched on a pile of planks and weed-covered rubble, they waited for the school party to disembark at the other end of the station and climb into the waiting pay train. Every now and then Benny looked nervously round the corner of the hut, until Tucker ordered him to knock it off.

'Just relax,' he said. 'We'll hear that train going. They make a fantastic noise when they blow out. Keep your head down.'

To while the time away he got out his pack of cards from his anorak pocket and the three of them settled down to play. They soon got so taken up with the game that they barely heard the local train start up and pull out. In fact, Tucker was just about to deal out another round when a quiet Welsh voice made them jump right out of their Y-fronts.

'You boys haven't missed your connection, have you?'

A tubby little man in a faded guard's uniform, cap on the back of his head, was looking down at them.

'You are with the camping party that's just changed trains aren't you?'

Tucker was on his feet, talking fast and smoothly.

'Oh no. We're waiting for the next train for London.'

'Oh yes? Well, you'd better make yourselves comfortable, boys. It's not due till 2.30.'

'But, that's ...'

'... tomorrow morning. It's the mail.'

'You're kidding.' Tucker's voice, no longer smooth, went up an octave.

The railwayman smiled, an amiable, gap-toothed grin.

'We've two trains each way stop at the Junction by day, and one by night. The day trains have gone.'

'Oh no.' Alan and Benny were on their feet, glaring at Tucker. What had the idiot done to them? But Tucker kept cool.

'Ah well, in that case. We'll have to go by road. Where's the nearest ...?'

The smile broadened. 'The A-4's about five miles that way.' He walked along with them to the exit by the little station house, and pointed up a narrow, tree-bordered lane. Then, holding out his hand, he said, 'I'd better have the outward half of your returns, hadn't I?'

'We were on the group ticket,' said Tucker desperately.

The guard shook his head, slowly. 'Playing hookey, eh?'

'Hookey?'

'Or, what do they call it now – bunking off, boy?' He let them pass through the gateway into the station yard. Then he pushed his hat further back on his head and said, 'I've never heard of anybody playing truant on holiday.'

Two hours later Tucker and his men stopped under a tree by the side of the road. The rain had started again and the clouds, if anything, seemed thicker. Their anoraks kept off the worst of the rain, but a lot had trickled down on to their trousers and down into their socks. Benny's plimsolls had begun to squelch and Tucker was sure he had a blister.

'Well,' said Alan aggressively. 'Where's the A-4? You've made a right cock-up of this, haven't you?'

'Listen,' said Tucker. 'Just trust me, right? We keep going north like this, we're bound to strike the A-4, and that goes east-west. We can't miss it. Pick up a lift and we'll be in town by evening.'

'How d'you know we're going north?'

'Well, we got a fix on the sun an hour ago, didn't we?'

'How d'you know it was the sun?'

'Oh give up will you.'

'How d'you know the A-4 runs east-west?'

'Well, course it does.'

'It could run south east north-west in bits. It's not a motorway.'

Tucker glared at the two of them. 'Come on. It can't be more than a mile up here.'

Alan put down his rucksack. 'I'm not moving. What's more, I'm hungry. My stomach's rubbing on my backbone. So get your rucksack off and let's eat. You've had my stuff and Benny's.'

'Er –' said Tucker.

The two of them suddenly jumped on Tucker, rolled him on the wet grass, and stripped off his gear as though they were skinning a chicken. Alan jerked the cords and pulled open the rucksack top. Then with utter lack of consideration he began to throw Tucker's clothes this way and that. At last, with a gleam in his eye, he delved down and held up – a bag of crisps.

'This was all you had,' he accused.

'I was going to lay on a supper at the chippy tonight,' said Tucker quickly.

Alan tore open the bag, dumped half the crisps in Benny's open palm and stuffed the rest in his own mouth.

'Now, get your gear packed,' he said sternly. 'And the

next house we come to, we're asking the way to Fawley Whatsit – we're going back to camp.'

'You're mad,' said Tucker. 'Baxter'll string you up. Playing him along. And telling that bloke we were from Brookdale.'

'*You* did that,' exploded Benny.

'Well, it's done now isn't it? Listen, if we keep on along this road, we're bound to come out somewhere. Then we get a lift and ... Come on,' he added, 'the rain's stopping.'

Without a word, Alan and Benny swung up their rucksacks and set off along the road.

Tucker was right. After about half an hour they did come out somewhere. They came to a cross roads, with a signpost saying 'Welbourne Junction' on one arm, 'Fawley Grange' on another and 'To the A-4 and Gloucester', on the third. The fourth arm was broken off. The trouble was the whole issue was lying on its side in a ditch. Tucker looked up at the sky.

'Hey,' said Benny sarcastically. 'Isn't that the moon up there?' Tucker made a lunge at him, but his heart wasn't in it. 'Let's turn right,' he said. 'I think that's north.'

The others said nothing, but humped up their packs and marched on. Tucker had the feeling that a beautiful friendship was slowly dying. He set off behind them. His feet were killing him. He was sure he had a blister on the other one now. What's more, it had started raining again.

They had not marched more than half a mile down the turning, when Benny pointed ahead and shouted.

'Look, there's somebody.'

'It's only a kid,' said Alan.

'Makes no difference, he must know where he is. Hey, kid,' shouted Benny and began to run after the figure ahead of them. Tucker and Benny lumbered along after him. But just as they came close, they saw that the lad was dressed in an anorak and carried a rucksack like themselves.

'Cor, a flipping hiker,' said Tucker. 'Bet he's lost as well.'

At the sound of his voice, the boy turned round.

'Hey,' said Alan, 'that's one of the first years isn't it? Hey, what are you doing here?'

But the kid took one look at them and began to run as fast as his feet would take him.

# Chapter 11

Alan speeded up, passed Benny and began to overhaul Duane. 'Hey, what's up?'

But Duane, instead of slowing down, began to duck and dodge blindly. But there was nowhere for him to go and in a matter of seconds the three of them had cornered and grabbed him. He struggled for a moment, then stood still. Alan looked in amazement at the dead-white, tear-stained face.

'Where do you think you're going?' he demanded. Duane bit his lip and shook his head.

'Well, he's bunking off, that's for sure,' said Benny.

'If he is, he's not coming with us,' said Tucker. 'We can't take him with us. We'll be lumbered.'

Alan turned on Tucker. 'You stupid – We can't leave him. He's got to go back to camp.'

'Oh yes. And are we going to take him there?' asked Tucker sarcastically.

'I am, anyway,' said Alan. 'What's more, he must know which way it is. So if you want to go up to London, be my guest. I've had enough. I'm going back to camp.'

'And me,' said Benny. 'Come on,' he said, taking Duane's arm. But to Benny's surprise, Duane threw off his hand and made a break for the road again. Alan reached out a large arm and barred his way. Duane swore, then sobbed. Alan put his arm round the boy's shoulders.

'What's up? What d'you want to bunk off for? Has somebody been on to you? You tell us and we'll . . .'

A violent shaking of the head, more sobs burst from Duane. Alan bent his head down, then looked baffled.

'You what? Airfield – what about the airfield?' He listened carefully, the look of disbelief on his face growing. Then he turned to Tucker and Benny.

'Hey, Tucker, you're in the fourth division. He was going to bunk off for real. He thought he could stow away on the airfield next to the camp.'

'Dumbo,' said Benny. 'That airfield hasn't been used since World War Two.'

Alan nodded. 'He knows that now. He just ran out of camp.'

'So, he can just run back then,' said Tucker.

'I'll do you in a minute, Tucker,' said Alan. 'We're taking him back. You please yourself.'

'You'll have to carry him then,' said Tucker shrewdly. 'He's shattered. He'll flake out on you in a minute.'

Alan shrugged. 'OK. Look Benny, you take his gear.' He unslung his own rucksack and thrust it in Tucker's arms. 'Come on.' He took the unresisting Duane and hoisted him on his own back. 'Right?' He began to walk back to the crossroads, Benny walking behind and Tucker making a very unwilling third several paces to the rear. They reached the road junction, turned as Duane directed and marched on in silence.

This time their luck was in. Out of the drizzle suddenly loomed a moving shape.

'Hey, look,' yelled Benny. 'It's the school minibus.'

Indeed it was. At the wheel was the tall, fair-haired young man who had started the chapter of accidents earlier that day. Leaning from the side windows were Hopwood and Baxter. The minibus ground to a halt and the young man flung open the door, while Baxter and Hopwood leapt to the ground.

'Look,' the young man pointed. 'We're in luck. Those lads from Brookdale have found him.'

Baxter stared. 'Brookdale?' He advanced a pace or two, eyes fixed on Tucker, while Hopwood hurried forward and lifted Duane from Alan's back.

'No, Roy. Not Brookdale I regret to say. Grange Hill.'

Baxter turned to Hopwood: 'What price your fiver, eh?' Hopwood turned from helping Duane into the minibus.

'Oh, I don't know, it's early days yet. We're only on Day One. Another thirteen to go.' He climbed in, followed by the fair haired young man.

Baxter grunted. Another thirteen days like this? His eyes rolled skywards.

'Beam us up, Scotty,' he said.

'I beg your pardon?' said the young man at the wheel.

'Nothing. Just take us home, Mr Wilmot. I need my supper.'

# Chapter 12

*CAMP LOG: Day Two*: Grey overcast skies, wind south west, showers. Not very promising. All settled in though after *somewhat* disturbed night. Someone spotted bats in the scrubland up the valley and first years kept each other awake for hours with tales of vampires. Some ingenious person invented a ghost for the old airfield – a phantom pilot who flies at full moon.

Usual arguments over who sleeps in which tent. Roy (deleted) Mr Wilmot had guy ropes pulled up last night. Mr Baxter promises collective punishment if it happens again. He intends to run a very tight camp, with PT every day, cross-country runs and slimming courses (no names mentioned). No camp discussions or meetings, everything done by numbers at the blast of a whistle. That does not suit everyone. Still, should keep us warm. *That* will be a blessing.

PENNY LEWIS

# Chapter 13

Tucker woke with a tremendous sneeze. Where was he? He had a diabolical pain in his back. One end of him was warm, but the other was freezing cold. Somebody was pouring water over his face.

'I'll ...' he muttered, and opened his eyes.

He was lying half in and half out of the tent. His shirt, which he hadn't felt like taking off last night, was sopping wet. It was raining on him. He'd been lying on the grass for hours. He'd catch pneumonia. How did all this happen? Where did he go wrong? Slowly he remembered the events of yesterday, and groaned. He was a prisoner in Stalag 99. With his one open eye he looked out over miles of damp grass to the top of the hill where he could make out fence posts and barbed wire against the skyline. He *was* a prisoner in Stalag 99.

Slowly, painfully, he dragged the top half of his body back inside the tent. No wonder he had been pushed out. Three bodies in sleeping bags were piled up just inside, Benny, Alan and Doyley. How did Doyley get in there? Then he remembered: Baxter had put Doyley in last night to make up a four man tent load. When he'd protested Baxter had told him if he didn't like it he could go across to the other lines and share a tent with Trisha Yates.

Just then, he heard her voice raised in a shriek from the girls' tent ten yards away.

'Look at that. It's a snake.'

And Pamela Cartwright with her horsey voice answered, 'Come now Trisha. It's only a ridge-backed slug.'

'How nice! The flaming thing's six inches long.'

'I know. It's a very interesting specimen. Let's take it to Mrs Thomas.'

'You can have it for breakfast for all I care. Just get it out of here.'

Tucker scratched his head. Maybe Pongo wasn't so stupid after all. She hated camp. That showed signs of intelligence. The thing was, what to do? How to get out? They reckoned the village was three miles away. His feet still burned from yesterday's hike. Oh no.

Clang, clang clang.

Precious Matthews, her hair wild and glistening with raindrops, the hood of her anorak thrown back, marched past the tent banging on a saucepan.

'Hey, pack it in,' shouted Tucker.

She turned and looked down at him.

'You look like a disaster area,' she said.

'Just pack that stupid noise in,' threatened Tucker.

'You want breakfast, you get up. We finish serving in ten minutes.'

Tucker looked at his watch. It was five past nine. What day was it? Sunday. They couldn't wake people up at five past nine on Sunday. There must be a law about it. Human Rights. He'd write to President Carter.

An enormous weight struck him in the back, then rolled over him. Alan in boots and pyjama trousers, towel hanging from his shoulders, was staggering off to the wash-place. Tucker sank back, as Benny and Doyle clambered over and followed. Wash? They must be mad – cold water, open air wash-stands, latrines with a canvas screen and no roof and spiders running round your . . ., rain coming down and cold fried egg and a greasy sausage at the end of it. He was crazy. They were all crazy. Suddenly he felt hungry and grabbed for his plimsolls. Two minutes later he was crawling over the field to the mess room. He stared. Everybody was late for breakfast, even the teachers. A queue ran along the serving counter, a trestle table alongside the camp stoves, and round the inside of the hut. The place smelt of wet clothes. Euch. Tucker shuffled along, eyes closed. Someone further up began to sing, 'Why are we waiting?' Behind the serving table, Pogo Patterson, Christopher Stewart and Precious

42

Matthews, sleeves rolled up, butchers' aprons round their waists, ladled out the egg and sausage.

'No you can't have any more. One egg and two sausages each.' Tucker opened his eyes. That kid Stewart was throwing his weight about? He'd better not try it with him. The queue moved faster now. Plump Anita Unsworth had joined the servers carrying a huge tray of freshly fried sausages. Ah good, thought Tucker as he neared the counter, just right for me.

He heard voices behind him. Trisha was there, with Susi MacMahon. Further back he could see Benny and Alan. Idiots -- rather get washed in cold water than have a hot sausage. He took his full plate and headed for the tables. They were crowded. Was it going to be like this every day?

'Come on, Peter.' Miss Peterson beckoned him from the corner of the hut where the teachers were sitting. 'Sit here until someone finishes on the other table.'

Tucker sat down, eyes on plate, feeling Baxter was glaring at him from across the board. He started to eat. He was hungry. He'd have to get more bread.

As he headed back to the kitchen, voices were raised from the queue. Aggro? Tucker quickened his pace, then stopped as he saw what had happened.

Big Eddie Carver had pushed into the queue alongside Susi, and little Christopher Stewart wouldn't serve him. Carver leaned over the table.

'Listen, big mouth. I've got things to do. I'm helping run this camp, see. So stop being so stupid.'

Stewart stood his ground. 'I haven't had my breakfast yet either. I won't get it till all you lot have had yours. But nobody gets served out of turn. It's not fair.'

'That's right, get to the back of the queue,' came a voice from further along. Carver swung round and glared. Tucker knew it was Alan. Carver turned back and said to Stewart.

'Are you serving me or not?'

'When you get to your right place in the queue,' came the answer.

Tucker helped himself to bread from the box at the end of

43

the table. This kid Stewart was mad. Carver would have his egg and sausage first and eat him raw afterwards. Then he heard Susi's voice saying anxiously.

'It's all right, honestly. Eddie – he asked me to keep his place.'

Little Stewart shrugged: 'OK.' Carver glared at him and held out his plate. No more was said. But as he walked away, Tucker saw him looking along the queue, trying to spot who had shouted. Alan stared back at Carver, then turned to get his breakfast.

Tucker walked alongside him to the table.

'What you playing at, dimbo? Bodyguard to the first year?'

Alan raised his voice.

'Some people think they can do what they like. Well, they're mistaken.'

'Watch it, Alan,' muttered Tucker.

He squeezed on to the table alongside Alan and chewed his piece of bread. This camp wasn't just uncomfortable. It was going to be dangerous as well.

# Chapter 14

That afternoon, fed up with sitting in her tent watching the rain, or keeping clear of Baxter's keep fit session, Trisha Yates got her writing pad out of her rucksack and went over to the mess room. She might as well write a letter to Cathy. There was nothing else to do.

'Dear Cath,' she wrote,

I shan't forgive you for this for a long time. You must have known Sooty Sutcliffe wasn't coming, that's why you stayed away. All this garbage about your Mother not being well.

I thought about you last night at the disco with Neil while I was listening to the rain drip down the tent. This morning I found a foot long slug on the ground sheet, and when I went over for breakfast I put my foot in a cow pat – nearly ruined my white shoes.

Pamela Cartwright made some remark about unsuitable footwear – I could have strangled her. I expect I will before the fortnight's up. At least it'll make a bit of excitement.

What people see in the country I can't imagine. It's not even quiet. At two o clock last night I heard a scream, like someone having their throat cut. Cartwright says, 'It's only a vixen' – she would. Then at half past four the blackbirds start, and pigeons, on one note all the time. If I got two hours sleep altogether I was lucky.

Then, what did I see first thing? Baxter coming out for a shave in just his pyjama trousers, enough to put you off marriage for life!

Jenkins, Humphreys and Green and little Duane Orpington out of the first year tried to bunk off yesterday. They won't be the only ones.

Anyway, Miss Hargreaves, write us a long letter about all

you've been doing before I go slowly out of my skull.

Love Trisha

'P.S. 13 days to go.'

# Chapter 15

That afternoon, bored stiff and cold, Tucker, Benny and Alan pulled on their waterproofs and went for a walk along the stream. Ahead of them they could hear the first years yelling to one another and throwing stones into the water. Duane Orpington was there, but very quiet, not joining in the general mucking about. He seemed to have teamed up with Clare Scott, or rather she seemed to have taken him in hand. The two of them were standing together, chatting and watching the others.

Tucker and his mates strolled on slowly. The going was heavy; great clumps of grass and potholes in the soft ground. Ahead were trees, and beyond a thick dark wood.

'Not much there,' said Tucker. 'Let's go up the other way and have a look at the airfield.'

'Not much there either,' answered Alan. 'I had a look through the wire this morning. All the runways are grassed over with bushes growing on them, trees and all. And the hangars all seemed to be falling down. They must have packed in using it donkeys years ago.'

'Still got the wire round, though.'

'Oh yes, probably going to put missiles on it,' said Tucker. 'You know – Pow – that was the world that was.'

'Well, thanks for that thought,' said Benny. 'This place is getting to you Tucker.'

'This place has *got* to me,' answered Tucker.

'Hey, listen,' interrupted Alan, turning back.

'It's only those first years by the water.'

'No it's not, it's something else.' Shrugging, Benny and Tucker followed Alan back along the stream, struggling over the uneven ground. As they rounded a bend, they came on the first years in a tight group at the top of the slope.

Some sort of row seemed to be going on. Christopher

Stewart stood a little way apart from them and beyond him stood Eddie Carver. Carver was choked, Tucker could see, like a big bloke always is when he wants to poke a small bloke one, but knows he's really too small to bother with, but can't stop himself anyway.

As they came up, Carver was saying,

'Listen Stewart. Don't ever do anything like that to me again.'

'Like what?' Stewart was scared but wasn't backing down. Precious Matthews moved up and stood alongside him. It looked as though she was going to get in between them. Her eyes were flashing.

'Like telling me to get to the back of the queue. Who d'you think you are?'

Carver leaned forward and then stopped as he suddenly saw Tucker and his mates.

'What do you lot want?'

Alan spoke. 'Just watching you, Carver. Think you're big enough to take Stewart?'

Carver's lips thinned.

'I'm big enough to take you, Fat-boy, and I will.'

'Any time, Carver.'

'Shut up,' whispered Benny. But Alan took no notice.

'Any time, *mate*.' Alan repeated.

Carver hesitated a moment, then decided to ignore him. He turned again to Stewart.

'Just watch it, that's all.'

By evening the incident had spread all over camp.

The rain had stopped and people stood around in small groups, waiting for supper, eyeing one another and talking amongst themselves. The teachers were already aware that something was wrong, but they were not sure just how far it had gone.

They soon found out in the mess room when supper began and the campers started to queue up. Christopher, Pogo, Precious and Anita stood behind the table, fiddling nervously with ladles and forks, shifting the hot serving pans to and fro.

'All right,' called Mrs Thomas, 'let's begin. We're all hungry.'

The queue began to move, the noise began, the banging of ladles on the sides of pans, the slap of mashed potato and greens on the plates, the shuffle of feet and scrape of benches as people sat down. Slowly people began to talk, the noise growing louder until the hut filled with the sound of chat, as people went over what had happened, or not happened, during the day.

The hush when it came spread from the kitchen through the mess room until everyone was quiet and looking at the counter.

Eddie Carver stood there at the head of the queue, holding out his plate. He wasn't saying a word. He waited. On the other side of the counter Christopher Stewart stood, arms by his side, ladle resting on top of the pan. At last Carver spoke.

'Come on.'

Hopwood rose to his feet and walked quietly over to the serving table.

Stewart spoke.

'We're not serving you.'

'What d'you mean, you're not serving me.'

'We're not – that's all.'

Controlling himself, Carver moved forward a pace and held out his plate to Precious. She stared at him, said nothing but slowly shook her head.

He moved on, Pogo lowered his eyes, said nothing, did not move. Anita turned red, half raised her spoon then dropped it again. All the people in the queue and at the tables held their breath.

Hopwood stepped forward and held out his hand. Stewart handed over his ladle. Hopwood took Carver's plate and went from one serving tin to another. Silently he handed the plate to Carver and just as silently Carver went to the table where the other sixth formers made room for him.

Hopwood turned round to the mess room.

'When supper's over, there'll be a general camp meeting. If it's still raining, we'll meet in here. If it's not we'll take the tables out and put them under the old oak tree. A little chat and fresh air will do us all the world of good.'

# Chapter 16

By the end of the evening the sky had cleared and the setting sun shone full on the thick foliage of the old oak. The campers crowded round the tables underneath, teachers and pupils packed in together felt the sun's rays on them and imagined they were warmer. The atmosphere was lighter too.

'Right,' said Baxter. 'That's settled. We'll have a meeting every evening under the tree, provided it's fine. And any complaints and disputes can be aired here. Anybody can speak, no need to be afraid. But if we all decide on something, then heaven help the one who doesn't fall in with it.

'What we don't want is people stirring things up. Everybody takes a little time to settle in. There are bound to be upsets. But don't take the law into your own hands. We'll all sort it out. OK? Now, one or two organizational points. Tomorrow we start the camp programme. And if your group is down for some activity you go on it. This is not multiple choice. Right?

'Now I understand some of you object to being turned out of bed at eight o'clock.'

'Hear, hear,' said Tucker and Anita.

'It's quite simple, really,' put in Miss Peterson. 'Breakfast finishes at nine. You don't get there, you don't eat.'

'OK,' said Baxter. 'We'll have a reveille whistle at 7.30. People on duty get a personal alarm call at 7.15. But otherwise no Butlin treatment. Just heaven help you if you're not ready to move off at 10 a.m.'

He looked round the tables.

'Any other business?'

'Yes, Mr Baxter,' said Roy Wilmot. 'As you know I'm making a film record of the camp, just the main items,' he

51

added hastily. 'I thought we should have a written account to go with it.'

'Penny's keeping a camp log each day,' said Susi MacMahon.

'Good,' said Baxter. 'She can work in with Roy – with Mr Wilmot.'

'I thought she wasn't supposed to write for the school magazine any more,' came a voice from the back.

'You have the kindest thoughts, Doyle,' replied Baxter. 'Rest assured that Miss Lewis's log will only become the official record of the camp when we have all accepted it.'

Roy Wilmot spoke: 'There are lots of things I may miss. I can't be everywhere. So if anyone takes still pictures, can I please see them – if they're not private, that is? They'll help to fill in the gaps.'

'OK?' said Baxter. 'Who's got a camera?' Several people raised their hands. Tucker noticed that Doyle did not. He looked at him and Doyle looked away. What was the Boil up to, he wondered.

'Before we break up,' put in Mr Hopwood, 'there is one thing I want to raise with this meeting.' He held up a crumpled piece of notepaper. 'Someone put this on the tree last night. I found it this morning. It's hand-printed. The writing looks shaky, as though someone's trying to disguise it.'

'Come on sir, what does it say?' came a dozen voices.

Hopwood grinned, then read: 'Prevailing wind south west. Move the latrine pit across the field or you'll regret it.'

There was burst of laughter. Hopwood asked, 'Is anyone going to own up?' There was silence. He glanced round. 'Just as you like. But in future, any more notices on the tree, they'd better be signed so we know who is giving the instructions.'

'Right,' said Baxter, 'I declare this parliament adjourned.'

When all the others had gone, the staff sat on round the table. Mrs Thomas looked worried.

'I'm concerned about Duane. I know he didn't get very

far, but he intended to run right away, didn't he? Oughtn't we to let his parents know?'

Terri Mooney shook her head. 'Home – I mean his father – is the reason. If we tell him, Duane will be in real trouble when he gets back. I think we just have to keep a close eye on him, that's all, just make him feel he's among friends.'

Miss Peterson smiled: 'Clare Scott seems to have taken him in hand. They've been roaming around together everywhere.'

'Ah, well,' said Hopwood, 'here's hoping he'll settle down and enjoy camp. His home set up is a long-term problem. We're not going to solve it here.'

'Right,' said Baxter, getting up from the table. 'The sun doth set. Who's on purity patrol?'

Roy turned faintly pink. 'I am.'

'Off you go, then, Roy. Watch the third year girls don't try and drag you inside. It'll be a fate worse than death. Just make a couple of circuits then come back up to the mess hut. We'll have your cocoa ready.'

# Chapter 17

*CAMP LOG: Day 3*: No rain today. Everyone more cheerful. First party down river for canoeing. Star of the day was Anita Unsworth, who took to canoeing like a duck to water (if you'll pardon the expression). But near disaster when Anita and Pogo Patterson tried to follow Precious Matthews and Christopher Stewart under one of the crank-up bridges with only 18 inches clearance. Mr Hopwood and Gary Hargreaves had to wind up the bridge to let them out. Rumour has it Pogo and Anita now have their names down for Mr Baxter's slimming course.

Blue sky and bright sunshine in afternoon. Temperature up to 19 degrees (68 Fahrenheit) and getting warmer. Wind still south west. Atmosphere in camp becoming thicker. Whoever wrote the mystery notice about the latrines was *right*.

PENNY LEWIS

# Chapter 18

'That does it,' said Tucker, collapsing through the tent door on to the groundsheet. 'Frying two million lousy sausages I can stand, peeling three tons of spuds I can stand, but not re-digging flaming latrine pits.'

'Had to be done,' said Alan, 'the whole camp would have been stunk out with the wind in that direction.'

'Too right,' said Benny. 'This morning when I woke up I wondered what had hit me when I stuck my nose out of the tent.'

'I thought it was Doyley's socks,' put in Tucker. He looked round. 'Where is he, anyway?'

'Don't know,' answered Alan. 'Never around when we were working. What do you think he's up to?'

'Don't know, but he's up to something with that camera, but what it is, who knows? Hey, and why did he keep his mouth shut when they were asking about cameras at the meeting last night?'

Tucker crawled across the tent floor and began to root around in Doyle's gear.

'What're you after?'

'See if he's taken any film yet.'

'Maybe he's got one of those cameras that develops the prints as you go. Be just like him.'

'So, he should have some pictures in his gear then, shouldn't he?' Tucker carried on turning Doyle's clothes over, then spread his hands out. 'Nothing here. Clean.'

'Anyway, Tucker,' said Benny, 'leave it now. S'long's Boily keeps off our backs, why should we worry?'

Tucker scrambled up. 'Listen, we've been slaving all day. Time for our break. Let's go down town.'

'Town? You're joking. Three pubs, the Co-op and a crummy little caff.'

'Best we've got. Anyway it's about time we looked the local talent over.'

'Talent?'

'Yeah, who knows. Could be entertaining.'

'And we could get our heads kicked in by the local yokels.'

'OK, if you're chicken, what can I do? I'll go on my own.'

'You going to walk all of three miles?'

'Beat it. Wilmot's taking the waggon down shortly. He doesn't know it, but he's going to have some help with the groceries.'

'Baxter says we shouldn't go in the shops in too big a bunch, the local custom gets stroppy if they have to wait for service.'

'Who says we're going in the shops? Let Wilmot do that.' Benny climbed to his feet. 'What have we got to lose?'

Half an hour later, the mini-bus rolled down the quiet streets of Fawley. Leaving Mr Wilmot to do the camp shopping and promising faithfully to be back in half an hour, the three ventured out into the main street. The skies were now clear and the sun shone down warmly. They strolled leisurely down one side, past the bank and the White Hart, now shut up for the afternoon. Further down the pavement ended in an open space with a market cross and a bench, where two old men and a dog were sound asleep.

'Hey, this is great,' said Benny. 'Really makes the camp look like the back of beyond.'

'Hey look, the Law,' said Alan.

'Where?' Tucker turned round in mock alarm.

Alan pointed to a white wall over which showed the tops of apple trees. Next to an iron gate a police plaque was fixed – the other was loose and the sign of the law hung sideways drunkenly.

'Flippin' 'eck, PC Plod himself. I wonder what he looks like?'

Tucker braced himself on the pavement feet astride, hands behind his back and roared. 'Hello, hello, hello.'

One of the old men on the bench woke up with a start and looked round wildly. Tucker creased up and staggered across the road laughing, followed by Alan and Benny. The old man stared after them and then slowly lapsed into sleep again.

'Here's the caff.' Tucker raised himself up and peered over the curtains in the window. He turned and grinned at Benny, then facing inwards again, he raised fingers to his mouth and did a gorilla face at the glass. From inside the cafe came the sound of giggling. Tucker smartly turned right and marched in through the cafe door, with Benny and Alan following him sheepishly.

Seated at the table across from the door, next to the counter, were two girls, one thin and blonde, the other plump, snub-nosed with reckless eyes, one green and one brown.

'Hello,' said Tucker.

'Hello,' said the girl with the reckless eyes. Then she spotted Benny and turned to her companion.

'Ooh, isn't he gorgeous. Come here,' she said. 'Oh, I'll have you wrapped up and sent home, I will.'

'I'd sooner have his big friend,' said the thin girl. 'He looks so masterful.'

Alan swaggered to the counter and ordered coffee.

He turned to Tucker: 'Why don't you go and help Mr Wilmot with the shopping, sonny.'

'Get off. Who made the introductions?' answered Tucker, lowering himself into a chair next to the girls. He waved his hand. 'My name's Peter. These are my friends Clarence and Montmorency. They're out on licence. I have to get 'em back by four o clock every day, but I can come out again later tonight.'

Green and brown eyes answered, 'I'm Lola.'

'You're not.'

'S'true. And she's Sandra,' she went on. 'Oh, I do like your little brown friend. He's cuddly.' She reached out and touched Benny's cheek. He jerked back and spilt his cup of coffee.

'Aw, he's shy. Which one is he, Clarence or Montmorency?'

'My name's Benny,' he burst out.

Lola turned on Tucker. 'Oh, I knew you for a liar as soon as I saw you.'

'Very intelligent of you,' said Alan. 'Listen, is there anything to do round here at nights?'

'Depends what you have in mind,' said Lola. Sandra giggled.

'Entertainment, I mean. Flicks or something.'

'Dah,' said Tucker, 'they haven't even invented the magic lantern round here.'

Lola ignored him. 'There's a disco over at Bexford tonight.'

'Hey, how far's that?'

'About ten miles.'

'Hey,' said Tucker. 'We'll get Wilmot to ferry us over.'

'You never,' retorted Alan. 'The only ferrying he'll be doing in down to the White Hart.'

A gleam came into Lola's eye. 'You boys want transport?'

Tucker nodded.

She turned and nudged her friend.

'There's someone we know who's driving to Bexford tonight, coming back from a job. He'll be driving past your place about eight o clock this evening.'

'How d'you know where we are?' demanded Benny suspiciously.

'Course we do. You're camping up at Hayes's farm, aren't you?'

'Listen, are you two going there?'

'We might be. Why do you want to know?'

Tucker raised his eyebrows at Alan.

'There's no answer to that.' He finished his coffee and signalled to his mates. They rose.

'See you at the disco,' he nodded to Lola.

'If we don't see you first.'

'Meet you outside if you like.' he added.

'Oh don't worry. We won't be able to miss you, if you

58

come in Ginger Joe's truck,' answered Lola. As they left the cafe the girls went off into peals of uncontrollable laughter.

By eight o clock, Tucker, Benny and Alan, in the best gear they could find, which was somewhat creased from being crammed into their rucksacks, were on the roadside by the camp field gate. The night was fine, warm even, and the few clouds were touched with pink from the setting sun.

'What did I tell you? Uncle Peter's fixed everything – disco, birds, wheels, the lot and all in five minutes,' said Tucker.

'Hey, here it comes,' said Alan, pointing down the road. Clattering and banging, an ancient green lorry, pumping out diesel smoke at the back, lurched to a stop. A teenage lad, pink-faced and ginger-haired, leaned out.

'You gentlemen want a lift? Well, hop in the back then. Sorry, can't take you in the cab, too much stuff in here from market. Can you manage?'

Tucker jerked up his thumb and the three raced for the back. They were barely over the tail when the truck shot away in a black exhaust cloud, throwing them into a heap on the floor.

As they picked themselves up and grabbed for the side, Alan said in a choking voice, 'Look at our clothes.' He turned round and banged on the back of the cab. 'Hey, stop, you maniac!'

Tucker held up his hands, made to wipe them on his jeans, then stopped just in time.

'Euch,' he said. 'What is it?'

Benny's nose wrinkled. 'If you don't know what that is you should never have left home. It's a flipping pig truck.'

All three of them now turned and banged on the cab.

'Stop the truck,' they yelled. But Ginger Joe drove on.

# Chapter 19

Darkness and quiet fell over the camp. The last shriek, giggle and groan died away. At the top of the field, in the mess hut, a tilley lamp perched on a trestle table threw a bright circle of light. Around the table, drinking mugs of cocoa, sat Baxter, Hopwood and Miss Peterson. Baxter shook his head, as one weary with the world.

'Which is worse? Having it pouring with rain and everybody stuck in the tents, or a fine day like today and them all running round causing general mayhem.'

'Oh, give me this gorgeous weather any time. Besides, it wasn't too bad when all's said and done, good game of rounders to end the day. All the small ones tired and happy.'

'Ah yes, tired and happy after stirring up the agricultural community.' retorted Baxter.

'What's this?' asked Hopwood. 'I've been out all day down the river.'

Baxter raised his hand and counted off on his fingers.

'One gate left open, six cows rampaging through the camp site, two tents knocked over and seventeen dainty feet dunked in cow pats. One very angry farmer.'

Hopwood laughed. 'Well that's normal.'

Baxter went on:

'Six First Years, with our resident Bolshies Stewart and Matthews in command, on a nature trail, spent the afternoon clearing timber and wire blocks from pathways. One very angry farmer.'

'Not the same one, I hope.'

'No, our reputation is spreading far and wide.'

'What was he angry about?'

'He blocked the paths up.'

'Well, he'd no business to,' put in Miss Peterson. 'It's a public right of way on the ordnance survey map.'

'Ah, but, Maureen, our little commandoes shouldn't ...'

'... take the law into their own hands.' finished Hopwood and Peterson. They laughed and even Baxter smiled grimly.

The door creaked open and Mrs Thomas came in.

'Cocoa in the jug,' called Miss Peterson. 'All tucked in?' Mrs Thomas grinned and nodded. She looked round. 'Where's Roy?' The others exchanged glances.

'On a mission of mercy,' answered Hopwood.

'Where?' she looked astonished.

'Called out from the White Hart by an urgent phone call. Could he please rescue three slightly smelly third years abducted in a pig truck and dumped in Bexford? Thought they were invited to a disco by the local talent.'

'Never underestimate the locals,' added Miss Peterson.

'Let me guess who,' said Mrs Thomas.

'Hm,' snorted Baxter. 'No prizes. Who else but?' He turned to Peterson and Hopwood. 'You two still betting on Jenkins?'

'Why not? Nothing disastrous has happened yet.'

'This is only Day Three,' said Baxter darkly.

'Nearly Day Four,' said Miss Peterson. 'I'm for bed.' She rose. Hopwood and Baxter followed.

'I'll stay and make some fresh cocoa,' said Mrs Thomas. 'Roy'll need a cup.'

'Keep your eye open for the phantom scribbler, then,' said Baxter, from the door.

'Ah, that. The First Years are convinced it's the airfield ghost. Duane's convinced he saw a mysterious figure among the trees behind the wire this afternoon. He's been keeping a close watch on the airfield. Now he knows it's a Second World War place, he finds it fascinating.'

'Duane's been in a very funny mood since he tried to run off.'

'Clare Scott was with him. She says she saw it, too.'

Baxter paused in the doorway. 'We'll just have to keep them all out of mischief for a day or two. No jaunts down town, plenty of activity.'

'We'll be all right tomorrow.'

'What's tomorrow? Remind me.'
'Pony trekking.'
'Good grief.'
'Good night.'

# Chapter 20

Twenty assorted ponies and twenty assorted human beings looked one another over next morning at the riding stables. The ponies kept their opinions to themselves. The human beings had more to say.

'It stinks,' said Benny as they trooped down the stable drive from the main road. 'Worse than Doyley's socks.'

'Not as bad as a pig truck, though Benny?' asked Miss Peterson, who walked behind them.

He flapped his hand. 'Nah. Hey Miss, have you ever ridden a horse before?'

'They're ponies, dimbo,' put in Tucker, who had reached the paddock fence and had straddled it in correct rodeo style.

'Get off,' said Benny. 'They're too big for ponies.'

'They're actually only about fourteen hands,' said Pamela Cartwright, who had followed them down the track with Penny Lewis.

'Fourteen hands. Looks more like four feet to me,' said Tucker, nudging Benny.

Pamela pretended not to hear him. 'It's a form of measurement. They barely come up to one's shoulder actually. Not really big at all.'

'All depends where your shoulder comes,' grinned Alan looking down at Benny. 'Still we'll give you a lift up, sonny.'

'As a matter of fact, he'd probably make quite a good rider.'

'He'd better. Because he's got a longer way to fall,' said Tucker, looking down from the fence.

'Well, we're all a bit raw,' said Miss Peterson, 'I've never ridden before.'

'You mean we're *going* to be a bit raw.'

Miss Peterson went on: 'I don't think any of us have done much riding, except perhaps Pamela.'

'Yeah, that's why she's dressed up like a dog's dinner,' said Trisha Yates, who had just arrived together with Susi MacMahon.

'Oh, you mean the jodphurs and riding boots, Trisha,' answered Pamela pleasantly.

Trisha pretended she hadn't heard and spoke to Susi in a loud whisper: 'Why people can't dress the same way as everybody else beats me. What's wrong with jeans? We're only going for a short trot up the hill, aren't we?'

'Will someone get that boy off the fence, please?' A large woman in riding gear had suddenly appeared round the corner of the paddock. She looked them over, her nose wrinkling slightly.

'Pity only one of you is dressed sensibly. Jeans aren't really the right thing. After the first couple of hours they tend to chafe a bit.'

'Couple of hours?' shrieked Trisha.

'Yes, my dear. We're going to break you in gently today,' brayed the riding school lady chuckling at her own joke. 'You'll be *rather* stiff and sore tomorrow. Bit like nappy rash if you know what I mean. But don't worry. A couple of days later when the skin hardens you'll barely notice.'

She clapped her hands together like a pistol shot.

'Gather round. We're going to saddle up first. Fiona and I will show you how.'

'I bet she will,' said Tucker out of the side of his mouth to Benny.

'Then you'll do it yourselves. Remember to make sure the girth straps are firm. We don't want you riding underneath like Comanche Indians.'

Fifteen minutes of general chaos followed, before the whole party was mounted and wending its way slowly up the hill track. Most people were cautious and let their pony make the pace. Michael Doyle, determined not to be tail-ended by Benny, pushed his mount forward and shoved

Benny's to one side. But that was Doyle's mistake, because in this game the ponies decided the order. Benny's mount reared slightly, dodged to one side and sliding up next to Doyle's pony gave it a sly side kick which sent it stumbling off the track and shot Doyle out into the gorse bushes.

'Kindly keep in line,' bellowed the riding school lady.

Doyle glared at her and staggered after his pony, which was nonchalantly cropping the grass further down the slope.

The others went on, and up-slope the going was fairly easy. The mounts took their time and the riders had a chance to get used to the motion. The horse's spine had an unpleasant habit of striking the base of the rider's with nerve-shattering impact just as the rider had recovered from the last jarring bump.

By and by everyone settled down, and as the ground levelled off and the view along the valley opened up to show bushes, trees and more hills to the blue skyline, they grew more confident. Tucker soon got bored with the gentle motion and tried to speed things up with a well-placed heel. To his delight, his pony responded and, on the open grassland, even broke into a trot. The group spread out, ignoring the calls of the intructor to keep station, and Tucker, feeling the breeze begin to rush past him, jerked on the reins and urged his pony on.

'Take it easy, Peter,' he heard Miss Peterson call, but she was soon left far behind. A mass of bushes loomed in front of him and he drew hard on the reins to guide his mount round them. It responded, but in the other direction. A few seconds later and he found himself going down hill away from the others at increasing speed, and to his sudden horror, he felt the saddle slip beneath him. The whole issue was revolving round the horse's belly and he was revolving with it. The beast was out of control. What was it John Wayne did, go round underneath and come up the other side? Or was that under a covered wagon? He couldn't remember. He couldn't think. He and the horse were parting company.

For a moment he was like Superman, in effortless motion through the air. Next moment he had landed, right on his bonce, and everything went black.

He opened his eyes. Funny, he could see two horses. There was his own with the saddle hanging half off it, and there was a second. Then he noticed the riding boots. His eye travelled up – fawn coloured riding pants, zip-up jacket. It was horsey Pamela, no less, beaming down at him.

'Are you all right – er Jenkins?'

'Ah yes, Cartwright, I think I am,' he responded sarcastically.

'The oldest trick in the world,' she remarked.

'What, falling off – I do it quite naturally.'

'No, the pony.' She turned to Tucker's mount and straightened the saddle. Tucker clambered to his feet as she gripped the girth strap and suddenly kneed the horse in the side.

'Hey, give over Boadicea,' he said. 'There's a law against that.'

'Not at all. You see the beasts sometimes inflate their lungs when you fasten the strap, then they breathe out and it loosens up.'

'On purpose?' Tucker's eyes opened wide.

'Of course. If you had somebody on your back every day, you'd think of ways of getting them off, wouldn't you?' She fixed the strap, tugged at the saddle and turned round to him. 'You have to show 'em who's boss.'

'All right, Mrs Thatcher,' grunted Tucker and advanced on the pony.

'Shall I give you a leg up?'

'No, ta,' he answered, and sticking his toe in the stirrup he made a mighty swing. But right at the crucial moment the pony shifted. Tucker's stomach hit the saddle and he slid off sideways with a groan, right into Pamela's arms. The two of them staggered sideways, tripped over grass tufts and fell among the bushes, rolling over and over.

Pamela was up first, hauling him up from the grass. But as he came clear of the undergrowth he heard a faint cheer from the hillside. Lined up on the rim of the hill like extras in a spaghetti western, were the rest of the riding party.

Pamela pulled free of him.

'Perhaps you'd better try again, Peter.'

# Chapter 21

'Never again,' groaned Tucker as he gently eased his battered body into his sleeping bag. This time he was at the top of the tent. If there was any rolling to be done, he was going to be on top. Doyle had been pushed to the open end. But funnily enough he didn't seem to mind. He was often nipping out during the night. Must have a weak bladder.

Next to him Alan grunted as he doubled up his legs and gently massaged them. 'Murder,' he muttered. 'And people do it for fun, and chase flipping foxes as well. They're bonkers.'

'What're you two moaning about?' said Benny from the depths of his sleeping bag. 'They always reckon the first day is the worst. It'll be better tomorrow. I enjoyed it.'

'Tomorrow? You're joking. Not ever again.'

'S'right. We're all out again tomorrow. The muscles loosen up, Miss Whatsit from the riding stables told me.'

'Oh yeah. Who's a little pet, then?'

'I wasn't the only one making friends, Tucker, was I? We saw you and Cartwright rolling in the bushes.'

Alan laughed and then squealed as his chest and back muscles protested.

'Too right. What were you up to Tucker?'

'I can't help it, can I?' responsed Tucker modestly. 'There's something about me. The women just can't keep their hands off.'

Ten yards away across the field, Pamela Cartwright sat half out of her sleeping bag, shining a bicycle lamp at the roof of the tent.

'You girls comfortable? Shall I switch off.'

'Comfortable?' grunted Trisha. 'You're crazy.'

'Poor Trisha. Would you like some of my stuff to rub on?'

'What, the stuff you use on the horses? Not flipping likely.'

'It'll wear off you know. The muscles loosen up after a day or two. Anyway, admit it, you enjoyed it a bit. Didn't you Penny?'

'Hm hm,' murmured Penny from the other side of the tent.

'I saw *you* enjoying yourself, Pamela, from the top of the hill,' chuckled Susi. 'Not that Jenkins is someone I'd pick to roll in the bushes with.'

'Oh, I don't know,' said Pamela, 'there's a certain primitive charm.'

'Yes,' answered Penny. 'Rather like dating an untrained Labrador.'

'Let's face it, all the blokes in our year are a bit immature.'

'Oh yes, MacMahon,' put in Trisha, 'we know your taste is for the older man.'

Susi blushed, and was about to retort when Penny interrupted quietly, 'If you ask me, you want to watch it with Eddie Carver. He's only got one thing on his mind.'

'Don't know what you're talking about.' Susi protested.

'Ha! She's just doing it to stir it up between fatty Humphreys and that Carver bloke.'

'No I'm not!'

'Oh yeah?' Trisha continued, 'We'll see.'

Susi was angry now. 'Can I help it, if Alan behaves like a big kid?'

'Boys can be a bit childish,' put in Pamela.

'Hark to the voice of experience. Anyway, MacMahon, you watch it. If there's trouble, they'll all blame you in the end.'

The tent flap was lifted and Miss Peterson's voice came from the opening.

'Sorry to disturb you, girls. But have any of you been out in the last ten minutes?'

'No miss. Why?'

'Just that someone's been putting up notices on that tree. And they've only just done it. You didn't see anything?'

'No. What did they say?'

'Never you mind. Good night all of you.'

'Good night.'

In the mess hut, the teachers sat round the table. A crumpled piece of notepaper lay in the centre.

Baxter read out slowly. 'They reckoned they were badger watching. That's their story. She's a bit old for it, isn't she?'

He looked round. 'They could be just inventing it, whoever they are.'

Mrs Thomas blushed slightly. Roy Wilmot turned scarlet. She spoke.

'Roy and I were out – the night before last. We were – looking for badgers. There's a sett in the woods downstream.'

Miss Peterson stifled a laugh, then she looked embarrassed.

'I'm sorry, that was unkind. But it is a bit bizarre. You know what the kids' imaginations are like. I mean we steal round every night making sure they are where they should be. We never think of them watching us.'

'What business . . . ?' Roy began to say then stopped.

'Afraid there's not much private life in school camp, Roy,' said Hopwood. 'After all we do get a laugh out of their antics. It must work the other way.'

'Except,' said Baxter, 'this isn't innocent fun. This,' he looked at Mrs Thomas, 'is downright insulting.' He cocked an eye at Miss Peterson. 'It's sexist even.' He paused. 'Somebody's stirring things up, and if I catch him or her, then God help 'em.'

Mrs Thomas spoke: 'The First Years are convinced it's someone from outside. They're quite hooked on this airfield ghost idea.'

Baxter shook his head. 'No, inside job this.'

'Well, that other notice about the latrines, that was someone who knew the area.'

'Hm. Anyway, I suggest we have a little night watch from now on.'

'We don't get much sleep as it is.' said Hopwood.

'Ah, just for an hour or so after lights out. I'll do the first turn tomorrow. And as I said, God help 'em.'

The tent flap was raised and someone stumbled over Benny.

'Who's that? Oh, it's you Doyley.'

'Hey, the phantom scribbler's been at it again. The teachers have been having a meeting at the staff room.'

'What's it say this time?'

'Don't know. Lot of old rubbish I expect.'

Tucker was awake. 'Listen fellers. I've got an idea. Could be a gas ...'

'What?'

'Fix the Phantom Scribbler.'

'How?'

'I'll work something out. Tell you tomorrow.'

# Chapter 22

In a quiet moment one evening, Trisha is writing a letter to Cathy.

'Dear Cath,

Just ridden another two thousand miles over the mountains. Beginning to wear the monster down. It's called Tarzan, believe it or not. I shared my packed lunch with him the other day. The sandwich spread set him back for a week – must have been the vinegar. He rolled his eyes, wrinkled his lips and nearly sneezed his head off. But he still likes me – I think.

What's the latest? After that roll in the bushes Jenkins and Cartwright haven't got anywhere. Probably not suited. The eternal triangle, MacMahon – Carver – Humphreys, is getting more dodgey. Hey, and something new. According to the Phantom Scribbler, Roy Wilmot – you know, the student – was out in the woods with – guess who? Mrs Thomas, the other night. Takes all sorts.

They still haven't caught him – the Scribbler I mean. In fact yesterday Miss Mooney was in charge of the kitchen; yes, you can guess. The shepherd's pie was a disaster, probably a very old shepherd. But she burnt three gallons of custard. Can you imagine the smell. Anyway, it was all thrown away and we had milk on the apple crumble, that was Pogo Patterson's idea. He's not a bad cook. Maybe blokes do have their uses.

Anyway, late last night Baxter was out on Phantom patrol. Some joker had turned the wet pit sign round the other way. We heard a big commotion and there was Baxter up to his armpits in bacon rinds, shepherd's pie and burnt custard.

They reckon Peterson was up half the night cleaning him down.

All for now. Why don't you write you miserable old – ? Doesn't anything ever happen round your way?

Love Trish

P.S. Only eight more days.'

# Chapter 23

The famous three had just got back from a canoeing trip and were assessing the damage.

'Water on the armpits, sunburn on the shoulders, cleg bites on the arms and blisters on the . . .' said Tucker, as he collapsed on to his sleeping bag.

'Could be worse,' said Benny.

Tucker took his plimsoll and carefully beat Benny over the head with it.

'What's that for?' demanded his mate, jerking away.

'That's for being cheerful. Now, say after me: "When Tucker is happy, everybody is happy. When Tucker is miserable, then . . ." '

Alan stuck his head in through the tent door.

'Hey, fellers, Roy's taking the wagon down to Fawley. Let's have a trip.'

'Get off, can't you see I'm dying?' said Tucker.

'I'm with you,' said Benny and scrambled up. Tucker made a half-hearted grab for him, but missed. Benny disappeared under the tent flap. Tucker lay back. His head struck something hard and he winced. Reaching back he dragged the object from beneath him. It was Doyle's sweater wrapped around something. He shook it out and a camera case shot across the tent floor, the flap bursting open as it rolled. A small print packet fell out. He reached out to open it. Now he could see what Doyle was up to, couldn't he?

'Leave that, Jenkins,' Doyle was in the tent doorway, scrambling over to him, hands out. Tucker jerked away, Doyle dived on top of him and the two rolled across the tent, slamming into the pole.

'Give over. You'll have the tent down!' Alan was in the doorway. 'Come on Tucker, stop playing games with your little friend.'

Tucker sat up, outraged, and Doyle took the chance to snatch back his prints, stuffed them into the camera case, gathered together camera and sweater and, ducking down, moved smartly out of the tent.

'Come on Tucker, Roy's waiting,' called Benny.

'OK.' Suddenly, Tucker felt like an outing and followed Alan to the waiting minibus. He could have a poke round Doyley's rucksack another time.

Twenty minutes later, leaving Roy Wilmot in the post office, looking at views of Fawley, Tucker, Benny and Alan strolled down the main street. It was like *High Noon*, just as hot and just as empty. From somewhere came the buzz of a hedge cutter.

'Think the sheriff is in town?' asked Alan.

'What d'you want to know for?'

'Because I'm hoping to meet someone, that's why.'

Alan led the way into the cafe. It was empty. They bought cans of coke and sat down. The air was stuffy and stale.

'Let's go outside and sit on the wall,' said Benny. The others followed him. The wall was broad and comfortable and the sun had warmed it. Tucker sat down and eased his back against a post so that he could see down the street.

'Hey Alan, who're you hoping to meet? No good going after Lola, she's Benny's bit.'

Alan shook his head. 'You've got a short memory, you have. I'm not forgetting I had a shirt and a pair of jeans ruined in somebody's pig truck, didn't I?'

Tucker sat up. 'That's true. Ginger Joe. I'd forgotten him. Think you can take him?'

'Think? I'm going to spread him all round Fawley, like pig –'

'I know what's wrong with you,' said Tucker slyly. 'You can't get Carver, so you're going to take it out on the pig-boy. Anyway, you're wasting your time. He's probably in the sty with his brothers and sisters.'

Alan shook his head and pointed.

Down the road on ancient bicycles, came two familiar figures.

'Hey,' said Tucker, 'Lola and Sandra.'

'No less.'

The girls stopped, leaned their bikes against the kerb and were on their way into the cafe when they saw Tucker and his mates.

'Ooh,' said Lola.

'Aah,' said Tucker, then asked cunningly. 'Seen Ginger Joe?'

Lola wasn't fooled. 'Oh, I don't think he's over this afternoon. Don't suppose we'll be hanging around either.'

She moved to pick up her bike but just at that moment, with a rattle and a shudder and a whiff of diesel, the old green truck lurched into the main road from a side lane and pulled up at the kerb. Tucker started to get off the wall, but Alan stopped him. The cab door opened and out jumped two lads, Tucker's age. He sized them up expertly. He and Benny could deal with them.

Could Alan handle Ginger Joe, that was the question?'

The cab door slammed and Ginger Joe came round the bonnet, pink face glowing with sweat above his dungarees. He looked even bigger than he had that night he'd shang-haied them to Bexford.

'Hello Lola,' he said, as if he hadn't seen the Grange Hill trio.

'Hello Joe,' she said. 'We were just getting along.'

'What for?' said Joe. 'Let's go in for a cup of tea.'

'That's right,' said Alan, getting off the wall. 'Let's all have a cup of tea, but a bit later. Let's sort something else out first.'

He stood in Joe's way.

'Don't they teach you manners in your school?' asked Joe. he raised a very thick, brown arm and put it in the middle of Alan's chest to push him out of the way. Tucker closed his eyes. There was a scuffle. Tucker opened them again and there was Ginger Joe bending down as if he were fastening his boots. His arm was up his back and Alan was gently

76

working it up and down like a pump handle.

'Now,' said Alan. 'First you say sorry to Mr Jenkins and Mr Green. Then we all go in and you can buy us a cup of coffee.'

'Like hell I will!' grunted Joe, as he broke free and his mates leapt at Alan from behind the wall. Lola and Sandra dropped their bikes and came closer. Ginger Joe's mates never reached Alan's back because Tucker and Benny reached *them* first and the entire ensemble rolled off the wall and into the gutter. Tucker's man was stronger than he expected and swiftly had him pinned down and was cheerfully banging his head on the kerbstone. But he was a fighter without imagination and was quite taken aback when Tucker's knee came up as if the doctor had tapped it with his little hammer. 'Oh mother,' he said and rolled off Tucker.

Benny had better luck. He was astride his opponent's chest in a flash, while Alan had Ginger Joe's boot in his grasp, using his leg as a lever to turn him over, nose into the dust. With a big heave, Alan let Joe relax into the gutter.

Then, looking round, he saw the cafe's rubbish bin, filled to the brim with sticky lolly paper and fag ends. He lifted it carefully from its stand so as not to spill it, and was just about to empty it just as carefully over Ginger Joe, when Lola gasped, 'Look out, lads!'

The sound of the hedge cutter had stopped. The iron gate in the wall of the constabulary had opened and out stepped the biggest man Tucker had ever seen in his life – seven foot high, fat, red-faced and white-haired, in a white shirt and black regulation trousers. In his hands gleamed the long-bladed hedge cutter.

'That's PC Hodges,' said Lola, by way of introduction.

# Chapter 24

'Look at that,' whispered Benny, 'The Incredible Hulk'. As the enormous copper advanced slowly across the main road in the sunshine, the all-in wrestling group began to break up. Alan gently stopped twisting Ginger Joe's leg and let it drop. Benny slid off his victim's chest and started to tip-toe across the pavement. Tucker was already stealing softly away. The opposition was on the move too, one of the lads very ungallantly reaching for Lola's bike.

'Right where you are!' came a bellow from the man mountain, who was only a few yards away now, the savage blades of his hedge cutter still raised in the air.

'Blimey,' thought Tucker. 'Maybe they execute you on the spot in this area.' But he didn't wait to find out. 'Come on,' he whispered out of the corner of his mouth to his mates, while sliding sideways along the cafe wall, with the skill of long practice.

He'd reached the corner when he realized he was alone. Benny and Alan had been nicked. Wondering why he did it, he turned back to join the others.

'Right, get lined up.' The order was unmistakeable.

Tucker, Benny and Alan stood in a line in the road. Tucker suddenly realised how hot it was. After all that exertion punishing Ginger Joe's army, the sweat was running off him.

'You lot are campers, aren't you?' Hodges wasn't really asking questions. 'Well, you're going back to camp and staying there.'

'We've got transport, sir,' said Alan hesitantly.

Something like a grin spread over the huge red face of the Law. 'I know you have. Shanks's pony.'

'But it's three miles.'

'Two and three quarters, to be precise. While you're walking you can think about it, for next time.'

'But mister, they . . .' Benny was about to protest. But PC Hodges had already turned to the opposition.

'And you lot get fell in behind!'

'We live here,' said Ginger Joe, indignantly.

'Do you?' came the reply. 'One more word out of you, lad, and you get marched back up to your Dad's place at Fawley Top – and that's seven miles.'

Ginger Joe said no more, but lined up behind Alan. His mates brought up the rear.

'And you can just put your bicycle down and join in.' PC Hodges was remorseless. Lola and Sandra sheepishly followed suit.

Suddenly a thought struck the Law. 'Now you lot can take out your shoelaces.'

Ginger Joe objected: 'You can't have our shoelaces *and* march us out of town, Mr Hodges.'

'Are you trying to teach me my job?' demanded Hodges in a voice that rattled the windows of the cafe. 'Get moving. Left, left, left.'

As the miserable crocodile, sweat streaming down their faces, wound its way down the main street, Hodges returned to his garden, disposed of his cutter and emerged a second or two later, wheeling his bike. Gently easing himself into the saddle he followed the procession down the road, roaring 'Left, left, left,' as they went.

Outside the Post Office, Mr Wilmot, seated at the wheel of the mini-bus, looked on in amazement as the Grange Hill trio and their ex-enemies passed by. Shaking his head, he let in the clutch and followed at a discreet distance.

The crowds assembling before supper near the camp mess hall stared in amazement, too, as the cavalcade approached. As it reached the gate of the camp ground, the campers were already streaming down the slope to get a closer view.

First came the three musketeers, pink faced and limping, shirts dark with sweat, then the locals, in no better condition, with Lola and Sandra somewhat in the rear and stumbling on their raised heels. Behind them, puffing gently

79

as he cycled slowly along, still in shirt sleeves, but with his helmet officially on his head, came the Law. And twenty yards further back, the school mini-bus with Wilmot driving.

'Halt!' came the command. The campers made a space as the arrest party stopped and stood swaying on the turf near the tents.

PC Hodges dismounted and turned ponderously to the crowd.

'Now, who's in charge, here?' he asked.

Penny Lewis was alone in her tent, writing up the Camp Log for the day, when she heard the commotion outside. There hadn't been much to report, to be honest. One party on nature trail, another canoeing and a third pony trekking. The weather had been fine (temperature 21 degrees), the wind light, south easterly. In fact it had been like that for days now and Penny had to admit that apart from one or two items (speculation mainly) about the Phantom Scribbler, her log had become, to say the least of it, boring. A yawn, let's face it.

Puzzled, she got to her feet and looked outside. In the space between the tents in the next line, she could see the crowd gather. And there was Mr Baxter arguing with a large policeman.

Putting down her log book and picking up a small note-book, she pushed her way out of the tent and began to walk round the lines to the camp entrance. But as she walked she was suddenly aware of a strange sound, not coming from the crowd across the field, but from nearer at hand. A kind of clicking noise. Once, twice, three times it came. She stopped and looked round.

Out of the corner of her eye almost, she spotted it. The back flap of one of the tents was slightly pushed back and poking out through it was the unmistakable black circle of a camera lens, telescopic by the look of it. Someone was taking pictures, and from cover, too. Why?

After a second's hesitation, she turned and stole back to

the other side of the tent where the cameraman was hiding, keeping one eye on the tent corner to make sure he was still in place. But that was a mistake, because not looking where she was going, Penny suddenly sprawled over the guy ropes.

She was up in a flash and round to the front of the tent, pulling open the door flap. But the tent was empty save for the usual jumble of rucksacks, jeans, tee-shirts, sleeping bags and underwear, scattered around the floor. This was a lads' tent, Jenkins and his friends, she knew. She paused for a moment and then crept inside. She didn't like to start turning things over, but a careful glance round showed there was no camera or similar gear concealed there. Penny pursed her lips. What to do? She couldn't start searching the tent just because she thought she saw something suspicious, could she?

The tent flap behind her was pulled back.

'What are you doing here, Lewis?'

She scrambled to her feet. It was Michael Doyle, smiling in his charming way.

She pushed past him without a word into the open air. The crowd by the camp gate had dispersed. From the top of the field came the bang bang of the saucepan call for supper.

As Penny hurried over the grass she heard Doyle shout.

'You keep out of our tent, Lewis. We don't want your sticky fingers in our gear.'

Clenching her fists, Penny ran to the mess room.

# Chapter 25

Supper had lasted longer than usual that evening and the usual camp meeting under the oak tree had been abandoned. The campers had gone back to their tents, some to rest their aching feet and limbs in their sleeping bags, others to chatter, going over the events of the earlier evening.

In the mess room, Roy had lighted the Tilley lamp and the staff and sixth formers were seated round one of the trestle tables, drinking tea. Baxter at the head of the table grinned amiably at Hopwood.

'I have to admit it Dan, that was something of a stroke of genius, inviting the Fawley kids – and the Law – to supper.'

'I have to admit you're right, Geoff,' answered Hopwood modestly. Then, more seriously, 'I was afraid it was going to be very nasty. I know Jenkins and his mates are a pain in the body public, both home and abroad, but I took exception to that forced march.'

Miss Peterson shook her head. 'I'd have agreed with you, Dan, if he hadn't included the local people as well. There's a kind of rough justice there.'

'And the girls, too,' added Mrs Thomas, 'it's clear they were stirring it up.'

'And now,' put in Miss Mooney, 'they're all thick as thieves.'

'Too right,' said Roy. 'I saw that big ginger-haired lad – Joe they called him – getting very close to Trisha Yates after supper.'

'What kind of a marriage would that make?' asked Miss Peterson.

'I don't know if his intentions towards Trisha are honourable,' said Baxter, 'but if I can get you all back to business, Ginger Joe has solved our problem for the expedition camp. That place of his Dad's up at Fawley Top sounds ideal.'

'Bit late in the day,' said Hopwood dubiously.

'Rubbish,' answered Baxter, 'we've still time for everyone to have an overnight stay there – go up one morning come down the next. Ideal. Keep 'em all out of mischief and complete the toughening up process. Apart from which, we're beginning to run out of things for 'em to do.'

'I think they're all busy with their own things now,' said Mrs Thomas. 'The Fawley kids promised to show them a swimming place at the Mill Pool downstream tomorrow.'

'All the more reason for an expedition camp. They'll just go soft, lying around in the sun all day. And Jenkins and Co will find some new diabolical scheme.'

'Ah come on, Geoff,' protested Miss Peterson, 'don't overdo the outward bound lark.'

Baxter leered at her. 'Aren't you worried you're going to lose your five quid over Jenkins and his mates?'

'Get away,' she grinned. 'You've not suffered, has he Dan?' She turned to Hopwood.

'What? not suffered!' Baxter counted on his fingers. 'What has Mr Jenkins done? Bunked off once, one unauthorised trip in a pig truck to Bexford, riot in the Main Street in Fawley, brought back in the hands of the police. What has Jenkins *not* done?'

He smirked at the two of them. 'No, I consider by any standards that even if Jenkins, Green and Humphreys are little angels for the rest of the camp, I've still won my bet.'

Hopwood pushed out his lower lip. 'I'm half inclined to agree with him, you know Maureen. Unless, of course, Jenkins gives Geoff cause to be grateful for something, that might even it up.'

Miss Peterson smiled and sipped her tea. 'We'll have to see what we can lay on.'

Baxter shouted with laughter. 'Go ahead. I'm almost inclined to double the stakes on that.'

'What, you'll give us two to one if Peter gives you cause to be thankful before the end of the trip?' asked Hopwood incredulously. 'You're on Geoff, you're on. And in front of witnesses too.' He looked round the table.

Mrs Thomas tapped on the wood with her mug. 'When you lot have finished laying your bets, can we finish this meeting? Is the expedition camp on or off?'

Baxter looked round the table. 'It's on. I'll draw up a list this very night and pin it up in here tomorrow. Is everybody ready to lead a party?' He turned to Miss Mooney.

'Would you take one?'

Her eyebrows came together in a frown. 'What d'you mean, Geoff? Why shouldn't I take a party?'

'You'd be on your own and it can be a bit hairy.'

'I know what it'll be like,' she snapped.

'Sorry.' He spread his hands.

There was silence a moment, then Hopwood cleared his throat.

'There was one other point, wasn't there, Geoff?'

Baxter looked embarrassed. 'Yes, actually, there was. We've had some more notices on the tree, these past three nights.'

'Some? I hadn't noticed.'

'I know. I've been whipping 'em down smartish.'

'Let's see 'em, Geoff.'

Reluctantly Baxter drew out the crumpled sheets of paper from his pocket and spread them out. Everyone round the table leaned forward. The letters, printed in large, shaky loops, were difficult to read.

'I can't see without my reading glasses,' said Mrs Thomas. 'What do they say, Geoff?'

Baxter cleared his throat. 'There's one about kids smoking behind the latrines. I think it refers to Barker and Taylor in the second year. There's another, about third years sneaking into the White Hart. Then there's one which is nasty, an implied threat to Eddie Carver, better watch his back, it seems.'

'Oh, why's that, Eddie?' asked Miss Peterson. 'I thought your little dispute on Day Two had been forgotten.'

Carver turned red. 'Ah, there's nothing to it, Miss.'

'What's the other?' asked Hopwood, reaching across the table. 'Oh!' He put it down again.

Miss Peterson held out her hand. 'I'll read it out if you don't.' She held up the paper. 'She thinks he looks gorgeous in his Y-fronts.' There was stifled laughter from the circle. She looked round. 'It refers to the night I helped Geoff clean up after his unfortunate dive into the wet pit.'

'Ah,' said Hopwood, 'that's a relief. All a bit ridiculous.'

'No,' answered Baxter. 'I take it a bit more seriously. I think someone is stirring it up. I think there's more to it than juvenile jokes.'

'How do you mean, Geoff?'

'Well, camps are rather special things in school life. Pupils and teachers behave in ways they wouldn't normally. People outside don't always understand, in the way family doings aren't always understood by outsiders.'

'Still don't quite follow.'

Baxter took a breath. 'What I mean is that this is just another of those parts of school life that people, the public I mean, just get the wrong way round. God knows, Grange Hill gets bad enough Press. People are always willing to think the worst. Incidents, behaviour which to us inside the school, pupils and teachers, just seem normal, can be blown up to make it look as though we're running a cross between Fagin's Den and ... well, take this afternoon's little party.'

'That ended well enough, Geoff.'

'Yes, provided it doesn't get into the local press, then picked up by our local press at home: "Grange Hill pupils run riot in holiday town" and that garbage.'

'You think somebody's stirring it up. But who?'

Roy cleared his throat.

'Penny has been doing some investigating. She thinks it's Michael Doyle up to his tricks. But I'm afraid Penny's got a grudge against Michael. And his behaviour has been impeccable all through the camp. What's more, even Jenkins has left him alone. They're sharing a tent.'

'True, Roy,' said Hopwood. 'And I think Penny should be careful,' he added. 'I was told she had been poking around in one of the lads' tents today. That won't do at all. Discretion's what we need: that's why we haven't said anything at a full camp meeting, yet.'

'No,' Baxter tapped the table. 'We don't want everyone going round spying on everyone else. Let's just keep our eyes open.'

'You don't think it's someone from outside?' asked Mrs Thomas. 'This strange figure Duane and Clare say they've seen on the old airfield?'

'I'm afraid Duane's just trying to get attention, poor kid,' said Miss Peterson.

'Ah, well, that's one problem we won't solve tonight or the next night,' said Baxter. 'Let's pack it in, folks.'

The mess room emptied and Roy put out the lamp.

In the darkness under the trees by the airfield fence, a silent figure watched the teachers go back to their tents.

# Chapter 26

Precious Matthews stuck her head in through the tent door flap. 'Come on you idle men.'

Pogo and Christopher stirred in their sleeping bags and looked up.

'Swimming,' she said and cracked her towel like a whip.

Pogo struggled up. 'What about breakfast?'

'We've got sandwiches. Come on, it's lovely and hot. Let's get down to the Mill Pool before the mob get there.'

Christopher and Pogo began to get dressed. Duane followed them more slowly. Five minutes later they stood outside with the girls – Precious and one or two more. Claire Scott stood a little way off from them. Christopher looked up at the sky.

'Fantastic', he said. 'Come on,' he called behind him.

Duane came out of the tent and stood, hand on the tent pole.

'I'm not coming swimming,' he announced.

'Why not?' demanded Pogo.

'Cause I'm not.'

'You're just going to hang around that stupid airfield, aren't you?' said Precious and flipped her towel at him. Duane drew back and frowned.

'If I want to, I will. No reason why I should come swimming just because you lot want to.'

Christopher rolled his trunks up in his towel. 'Please yourself. Go and poke round the airfield if you want to – go and play war games.' He made aircraft noises and waved with his hand. 'Your trouble is you don't want to do anything. Ever since you came here you've done nothing but talk about flipping Spitfires and Lancasters and the war.'

'What's it got to do with you if he has?' interrupted Clare, coming forward.

'Because we have to listen to him all the time. His trouble is he thinks it was all one big game – Battle of Britain – dog-fights and flipping Kenneth More shooting Jerries down. He hasn't the faintest what it was all about.'

'And you know everything about everything don't you?' snapped Clare. 'That's your trouble Stew, you know everything. Otherwise you're all right.'

' 'Ta very much,' said Christopher. He turned to Precious. 'Let's go.' They moved off. When they were several yards away Precious turned and called. 'You coming, Clare?'

'No, I'm not bothered,' she answered. She turned and smiled at Duane. 'Come on, let's go and have breakfast. Then we can talk about what to do.'

Duane stood still. She put her arm round his shoulder and gave it a quick squeeze. 'Come on. Don't take it all so seriously. And don't get so narked with Stew. He can't help it.'

Slowly he allowed her to pull him across the grass towards the mess room.


Later that morning, they stood by the camp wire. Duane's face had brightened. His voice was more eager. He pointed through the light screen of bushes that grew just inside the fence.

'Look, see where the grass is short. That was where they used to take off. And those were the hangars where they kept the fighters and the bombers, I mean depending what sort of airfield it was. And that taller thing over there at the back, that must have been the control tower, you know, where they got the messages – bandits at six o'clock, scramble.'

'Bandits?'

'You know, German planes. And scramble means get in the planes and take off.'

'Duane,' said Clare, 'let's walk a bit.'

They turned and began to follow the camp wire round. After a hundred yards or so, the field ended and the woods began. There was a broken fence across their path.

'Shall we go back?'

'No, let's follow the wire round.'

'What for?'

'There might be a way through.'

'On to the airfield? Don't be stupid. We're not supposed to go through. Come on, let's walk down through the woods.'

'Please yourself. I'm going.'

Clare shrugged. 'All right.' They pushed on. Under the trees the undergrowth was tangled and the ground uneven. Patches of bramble and hawthorn bush growing right up to the wire blocked their path. Time and again they had to turn aside and beat a path round some obstacle to keep the wire in sight.

'It must go on for miles. And it's just old wire anyway. What d'you expect to see?'

'I reckon there's a place where he comes through.'

'Who comes through?'

'The ghost.'

'Oh, get off, Duane. You don't believe that, do you?'

'There's someone there. You've seen him as well.'

'We thought we saw him. Hang on,' called Clare. 'I'm stuck on this flipping bramble.' Duane struggled back through the bushes and helped her free. Both paused for breath.

'There's all those notices as well.' he said.

'Those. I think that's someone in camp messing about.'

'Oh yeah? Well, how did they know about the latrine pit and which way the wind would come from?'

'That could have been a different one.'

'Well they were all supposed to be in the same handwriting.'

Clare said shrewdly, 'Suppose the first notice was someone from outside, and then somebody inside just copied the handwriting?'

Duane had no answer for that. 'Well,' he said, 'so if that first one was from outside, who wrote it then?'

'The farmer, maybe. Look Duane, let's go on or go back.

I'm getting bitten to death by mozzies standing here.'

Duane pushed on through the bushes. 'Dah, the farmer's never been anywhere near us, except when he rounded those cows up that day.' He vanished from view behind a larger patch of blackberries.

'Wish these were riper,' said Clare, beginning to search beneath the leaves amid the red and green berries. 'Hey there's some black ones here. Duane!'

But there was no answer. She struggled round the bush. The woods seemed empty. The wire was hidden in the strands of a climbing plant. Turning aside she ran on, slipping and falling on the grass. 'Duane?' She called.

'Clare!'

She jumped. He was behind her.

'How did you get there?'

'I've been through the wire and came back.'

'How?'

Here, he pointed back to where the creeper had covered the fence. 'Someone's propped some sticks up to keep the wire back, you can get through easy.' He held out his hand.

'Want some?'

'What's that?'

'Raspberries.'

'Hey, wild ones.'

'Don't know. They're growing just inside the fence, a whole big patch.'

'Come on!' Clare turned and followed Duane to the fence. Getting through was quite easy and beyond the turf was shorter, the bushes much thinner. Duane pointed. Some twenty yards away were long, low, round-roofed buildings with broken windows.

'Nissen huts. That's where they used to live. Shall we go and look?'

'No, let's have some raspberries. Hey, Duane. These aren't wild. Somebody's been growing them. Maybe we shouldn't take 'em.'

'Ah, come on. They won't miss a few.'

90

They sat down on the grass amid the raspberry canes and began to eat.

'Hey, I was hungry.'

'Don't wonder. It's nearly lunch time, anyway. Flipping heck, it's hot.'

Clare, her lips stained red with juice, lay back and shielded her eyes. 'It's smashing here, isn't it?'

Duane eased back until his body rested on a fence post, then slid down to the ground. It was hot.

'Anyway,' murmured Clare from the other side of the cane, 'it can't be a ghost.'

'Why not?'

'Ghosts don't grow raspberries.'

She chuckled. 'I'm sleepy. Anita kept me awake last night, having nightmares. She reckoned it was the cheese pie we had for supper.' She mimicked Anita: 'My Gran says never eat cheese last thing at night.' Her voice trailed away.

Duane's eyes closed. The air was still, insects buzzed nearby. He was thinking to himself, I wish camp would go on for ever. The sun was warm on his face; a plane droned faintly across the sky.

Duane's head was drooping, when the faintest sound nearby made him jerk up again. Two yards away, looking at him across the raspberry canes, was a figure, a thin figure in blue with the sun lighting up the side of its face.

Above the faded blue tunic pocket was a line of coloured ribbon. The head was bare, and the face --

The face was ghastly -- dark and twisted, the mouth at a terrible angle, one eye vanishing in scarred skin.

Duane found his voice.

'Clare!'

'What's wrong, Duane?' she called.

'There's ...'

But the figure had gone. The sky and the ground were empty. There were the bushes, the trees, the nissen huts with their broken windows. But the apparition had vanished.

Now Clare was looking down at him. 'Are you seeing things?'

'There was a bloke. An airman from the last war. Standing right where you are now.'

'Duane. You're dreaming. Too many raspberries. Come on, let's go back.'

# Chapter 27

Late that afternoon, Trisha put her swimsuit on, rubbed herself with oil and dragged a sleeping bag out on to the grass. Making herself comfortable, she began to write another letter to Cathy.

'Dear Cath,

Writing this lying in the sun. Magic. Getting a fantastic tan. Been swimming every day this week. There's an old mill pool where the locals have fixed up a stage for fishing and diving.

What d'you know, I've learned to dive. And swim underwater. Dead easy when you know how. There's a local bloke – very helpful. He's red-haired, eighteen and called Joe. Still, we can't all be perfect. He's a farmer's son, so who knows I may settle permanently in the countryside.

Talking about the mature type, Humphreys got so wound up about Susi and Eddie Carver that a fight started the other night. Your Gary and Dukeson had to pull 'em apart. One of them would have crucified the other. I'm not sure which. Alan's got more weight, but Carver's dangerous.

What else? Bullet did the cooking yesterday, made a fantastic stew with beef and beans. Everybody was going round like an outboard motor for hours afterwards. *Blazing Saddles* had nothing on us. Now you know why they sit round in a big circle at camp-fires.

Three more days to go. Time's passed so quickly. To-morrow our lot goes off on the expedition camp, you know, live rough up the hillside, carry everything, grub, tent, the lot. Still, only one night and a day. We'll be up at Joe's farm, which is good. But our expedition leader is Mooney, which could be dodgy. Everything she touches goes berserk.

The Sixth Form people have made a barbecue pit, so tonight we have roast pig and dirty songs.

See you,

Love Trish

P.S. why don't you write? Doesn't anything happen down your way?'

# Chapter 28

The barbecue was a great success. The pork chops sizzled over the red-glowing charcoal and two Tilley lamps threw a circle of light round the campers as they sat in the open air near the mess-hut. Ginger Joe had driven up from the village with his mates; Lola and Sandra had biked up, and there was PC Hodges, another stroke of genius from Mr Hopwood.

They all sat and ate and drank beer and coke while the darkness closed in around them. One of Joe's mates had a mouth organ and they sang and sang until they all ran out of numbers. Then in the pause as the fire died down and campers hunted round for more fuel Ginger Joe turned cheekily to the Law.

'How about a song from Mr Hodges?'

PC Hodges spluttered on his beer and shook his head, but the campers began to chant.

'Hodges, Hodges. Sing, sing, sing.'

He rubbed his chin, cleared his throat and said.

'I only know one or two from when I was in the Army, and I don't know if ...' he glanced round.

'Oh, we're very broad minded at Grange Hill, Mr Hodges,' Mrs Thomas reassured him.

'We-ell, you'll have to join in the chorus. Tisn't all that difficult.'

'But get on with it,' muttered Tucker.

Hodges took another mouthful, swallowed, drew a deep breath and began. At first his voice was pitched too high, and the first years started to giggle, but after a line or two he had it right and roared out with:

'There was cheese, cheese,
Wafting on the breeze,
In the stores, in the stores.

There was bread, bread,
Hard as lumps of lead,
In the quartermaster's stores.'
He paused. 'Come on everybody, the chorus goes ...
'My Eyes are dim, I cannot see,
I have not brought my specs with me ...'
'I know this!' shouted Duane, 'My granddad sings it.'
'I have no-ot brought my-y specs with me!'
Hodges drew a breath and sang again.
'There were eggs, eggs,
Walking round on legs,
In the stores, in the stores.
There was ham, ham,
Mixed up with the jam,
In the quartermaster's stores.'
They yelled out the chorus. Hodges followed with another
verse and the campers joined in. Suddenly Hodges held up
his hand.

'If you're going to sing, sing together. That last one was
ragged, ragged it was.' He paused. 'Who's that still singing?'

All listened in silence. In the darkness, not far away, a
thin voice was singing, tunelessly, like a weird chant.

'What's that?'

The sound died away. 'That was up on the airfield,'
whispered Duane.

'Don't let your imagination run away with you, Duane,'
said Miss Peterson.

'Do you reckon there's a ghost on the airfield, Mr
Hodges?' persisted Duane.

'Ghost?' said Hodges. He shook his head. 'Poor old
devil ... leave him alone.' He looked round. 'You want to
keep away from the airfield, son.'

# Chapter 29

*CAMP LOG: Day Twelve:* Weather still incredibly fine and hot. Temperature 25 degrees. But air still and hint of thunder. Can't last. But hope storm won't break until after our party goes on expedition camp this afternoon. Miss Mooney in command.

Everyone still arguing about the Phantom Scribbler, though he's been very quiet for two days. Little Duane says it's the ghost of a Second World War pilot from the airfield. The others tended to poke fun of him until the barbecue party last night.

I *know* who Mr Scribbler is. And when we get back from Expo Camp, if we get back in one piece, I'm going to smoke him out.

PENNY LEWIS

# Chapter 30

Duane and the others stood around the mess hut after lunch that day.

'Come on, Duane,' urged Christopher. 'Come on down to the pool. Look at the way those clouds are coming up, black as anything. It's the last chance for a swim if that lot comes down.'

'There's tomorrow,' answered Duane, digging his toe into the grass and glancing sideways at Clare.

'No there's not,' put in Precious. 'It's that Treasure Hunt tomorrow. It's supposed to last all day, then we'll be packing up. Come on.'

'OK,' said Pogo, 'hang on a sec, I'll get my gear.'

'I'm not coming,' said Anita. 'My Gran says if you get struck by lightning when you're near water, it's worse.'

She turned and walked back towards the lines.

Christopher looked at Clare and Duane.

'I suppose you two are going poking round the airfield. You want your heads fixing.'

'Hey,' said Duane. 'You won't say anything will you? Bullet'll skin us if he finds out.'

Christopher waved his hand. 'Get off. You know we won't.'

When the two of them were left alone, Duane turned to Clare. 'Are you OK?'

After a second, she said, 'OK,'

'Let's go then.'

They walked quickly towards the lower end of the woods where the stream went through just in case any staff saw where they went. Then in the shelter of the trees they turned again, and moved stealthily up field again to the airfield wire.

Clare shivered. 'It's dark in here under the trees.'

Duane shook his head. 'No, that's the clouds coming up.' He pointed upwards. The sky beyond the trees had changed from blue to dark blue, and was darkening by the minute.

'Let's get a move on. We don't want to get caught in the woods if there's any lightning.'

They stumbled over roots and trailing brambles, scratching their legs and snagging the sleeves of their shirts. The air seemed to grow thicker and the sky moved downwards and grew more purply dark.

'Here we are.' They were by the airfield fence.

Outside the shelter of the trees, they felt a chill breeze steal over the open space of the deserted runway. The heavens over them were now dark to blackness and great hammer-headed clouds swelled up from the horizon.

'Quick, let's get over to those nissen huts.'

A jagged lightning stroke split the sky and a sudden wind whipped up leaves and shreds of grass. Without thinking any more they rushed across the open space to the low black huts with their broken windows stuffed with sacking. The wind caught a door at one end of the hut and swung it to and fro, wheezing and creaking.

Then came the thunder and the first drops of rain.

Taking each other by the hand, they hurried inside.

# Chapter 31

In the late afternoon, the Grange Hill mini-bus, driven by Hopwood, drew into the side of a dusty lane at the foot of Fawley top. Hopwood threw back the door and allowed the expedition camp party to climb down into the road.

'That was like an oven, in there,' gasped Trisha.

'Not much better out here,' answered Penny, looking up at the darkening sky.

Susi hefted her rucksack. 'These are murder. Did we have to bring all this gear, miss?'

Miss Mooney, pale-faced, climbed from the van.

'We have to have two tents, a stove and food, Susi. It's all been divided as fairly as possible. It's the only way to do it.'

'Oh, it's not too bad,' said Pamela, heaving her pack on to her back. 'Shall I give you a hand, Susi?'

'Give us all a hand and stop playing the big hero!' muttered Trisha.

Hopwood leaned out of the cab.

'Terri,' he said quietly. Miss Mooney turned from the others and moved over to the mini-bus.

'Are you sure you're OK?'

'Yes.'

'You look a bit pale, that's all.'

'Oh, don't fuss, Dan. Honestly, the way you people have been going on you'd think I wasn't fit to have charge of a tea party.'

'Terri, you don't have to prove anything.'

She looked back at the girls, 'That's what you think.'

He shrugged. 'OK. Listen. I'll be back at the foot of the hill at ten o'clock tomorrow.'

'So early?'

'Yes. Remember, we've got the Treasure Hunt – grand

finale. Everybody involved, big sweep of the whole area, show what we've learnt, etc.'

She smiled. 'Thanks, Dan. We'll be OK. See you to-morrow.'

With an effort she hoisted her pack on to her shoulder. Hopwood let in the clutch, drove the van up the lane, turned it and drove down again past them, waving as he went.

'Ready everybody?' asked Miss Mooney.

'As ready as we'll ever be,' said Trisha.

'Right. It's four miles to the top. And we'd better move, before the rain comes down.'

From behind them came the faint rumble of thunder and the first fat heavy drops of rain splashed in the dust.

# Chapter 32

'Look at that,' whispered Duane, gripping Clare's hand tighter.

Inside the long room within the hut, the darkness of the woods and airfield outside seemed even more gloomy, for little light could come through the grimy windows. The curved walls of the nissen hut stretched away from them on either side.

'Beds, all those beds,' gasped Clare.

On either side, at intervals of three or four feet were iron bedsteads, neatly aligned, and behind each one tall metal cupboards with flaking green paint. Here and there were torn and faded posters and pictures cut from magazines. The eyes of long forgotten movie stars gazed blankly down at them.

Clare let her breath go.

'It's like in those films. She took a step forwards and absent-mindedly ran her finger along the foot of the first bedstead.

She held up her finger: 'Look, no dust.'

'Yeah. There's no dirt on the floor, either. Someone's swept it.'

They took a few careful steps forward, looking back at the door, which still swung in the wind. Duane touched the second bedstead. It was clean, like the first. So was the next one. Their footsteps sounded loudly on the concrete floor. Above them the first raindrops began to drum on the corrugated iron roof.

'What's that?' Clare pointed.

'A stove, I think. There's a chimney going up through the roof.'

'Hey, was that all they had to heat with? It must have been cold in the winter.'

'Well, they didn't have central heating, for sure,' Duane laughed nervously.

Clare gripped his arm and pointed again.

'Look there, on the last bed, by the door.'

'It's clothes.'

They came closer. 'No it's not, it's like belts and stuff, haversack, you know, all the gear. And look, those buckles, all the brass, see how it's shining. It's as though someone had done it up this morning.'

They were now against the wall at the farther end. Another door, closed, was in front of them.

'Clare?' Duane was still clutching her hand. 'Do you reckon we've gone back in time, to how it was in the War?'

She shivered. 'Oh, don't say that. But it's weird, isn't it?'

'Shall we try that door?'

He pushed on it and the door opened easily, as if oiled. Beyond was another short passage and to either side more open doorways. Inside one stood another bed, with folded blankets and on the floor beneath, a pair of black, patched, but polished boots. On the other side of the passage the doorway showed a table, and a wooden chair. There were plates, a knife, a fork, and a brown, chipped enamel mug.

'That plate's still got food on it,' whispered Clare.

'Yes, I'm afraid I'm rather lax about clearing up, these days.'

They spun round and Clare gasped. Duane was silent, but not surprised.

He had seen this man before, that blue uniform, so threadbare it was almost grey, with the wings on the shoulders and the medal ribbons above the pocket. Now he could see, on the sleeves, three grey chevrons. And he could see that the thin hair, carefully smoothed on the narrow skull, was pure white.

'Who are you?' demanded Clare, eyes fixed on the twisted, awesome face.

Behind the airman, lightning filled the long gloomy hut

with a sudden brilliance and thunder rolled over the curving roof.

A smile touched the distorted lips.

'I'm a ghost.'

# Chapter 33

As the storm broke, Baxter was having a quiet kip in his tent, the first of his favourite afternoon naps he'd been able to have for weeks. One party was safely off to expo camp, a crowd, including two staff, were down at the mill pool, and the rest were lounging in their tents, playing cards and doing other more or less harmless things. He dozed the doze of the the just.

The first clap of thunder shot him up into a sitting position on his sleeping bag. A flash of lightning, a bare two second interval, and a second almighty roll, brought him to his feet. He looked out in amazement. On all sides the whole area from woods to stream, from airfield to road, was in semi-darkness, the thickest blackest clouds he'd ever seen were hanging right down to the tree tops.

'My Aunt,' muttered Baxter, 'send for the Ark.'

'Maureen,' he yelled, but Miss Peterson, pulling on a yellow rain cape, was already hurrying from her tent.

'Are you thinking what I'm thinking?' she asked.

'More so,' he answered. 'Listen, I think this is going to be a bad one – there's enough water up there to sink Fawley without trace, and we're too close to the stream for my liking.'

'Well?'

'I think we'd better do two things. Get everybody we can together. Go round and let down the flaps and loosen off the guy ropes. Then get the sleeping gear up to the mess-room and wrap everything else in the groundsheets.'

'What about the swimming party?'

'Mrs Thomas and Roy are with them. They should have the sense to come back double quck.'

Miss Peterson looked up as the first heavy drops fell on her face.

'I hope so, because they're under trees at the mill pool.'

'Anyway, let's get the kids moving.'

'Only first and second years, I'm afraid.'

'They can still shift gear.'

The noise of a motor came from the road.

'Ah, Dan's back from Fawley Top.'

'Shouldn't he go back and pick them up?'

'Why? He's needed here. Besides, they're OK, they're near the farmhouse – solid building. All we've got is this garden shed,' he gestured towards the mess hut, and began to hurry down the lines calling to the campers inside the tents, who began to tumble out shouting and squealing and pulling on jackets and anoraks.

There was half an hour's pandemonium, with kids and teachers running this way and that, stumbling over one another, issuing contradictory commands, arguing, but getting the job done all the same.

By the time the rain came down in earnest, blotting out the woods, the airfield fence and even the three lines of tents, everybody, including the swimming party who had swiftly retreated from the mill pool, had withdrawn into the shelter of the mess hut.

Half the dining hut space was now crammed with sleeping bags and other gear. The other half was crammed with steaming drenched humanity. Baxter stood at the hut door and looked out.

'Well, it should be all right. But heaven help us if we have to spend the night here. It's going to be togetherness with a vengeance, and I'm afraid probably freezing cold.'

He turned to Miss Peterson and Hopwood who were counting heads.

'Geoff,' she said.

'What is it?'

'Duane's missing, and Clare Scott as well.'

'Good grief. Where on earth have they got to?'

'Well, the others either can't or won't say.'

# Chapter 34

When the storm broke, the expo camp party were a mile from their goal at Fawley Top Farm. The rain came down with full force, drenching them from head to foot, and within minutes their already heavy packs weighed them down like loads of lead. They struggled on, but the going became steeper and the narrow road more rutted and pot-holed. The rain scoured down it, turning the centre into a running stream and they jostled one another as they tried to walk on the ever-narrowing solid ground on either side.

'We've got to run for it,' shouted Pamela Cartwright, and she set off at a run, followed by Susi. Trisha, feeling like a camel in a weight-carrying contest, was about to stagger after them, when Penny caught her sleeve and nodded at Miss Mooney who had dropped two yards behind. The teacher's face was white and her lips seemed blue by contrast.

They dropped back.

'You all right, Miss?'

She gasped. 'Yes,' but stumbled and almost fell at the next step as her foot twisted in a wheel rut.

Trisha glanced at Penny and without a word they each linked arms with Miss Mooney, the three falling into step like a rather ill-matched team of horses, and began to stumble together up the last few hundred yards to the farm-yard gate and the field beyond. The farmyard was a quagmire, and by now Penny and Trisha had almost to haul Miss Mooney along. It was as though she had fainted on her feet.

In the lee of the field wall just beyond the farmyard, Susi and Pamela were struggling with the wet folds of the first tent.

Pamela turned and glared at them through the driving rain.

'Where the hell have you lot been? Come and give us a hand.'

Miss Mooney leant against the wall.

'I'll be all right. I just want to rest a bit.'

Trisha slid her pack from her back, plucked the strings open and pulled out her groundsheet. She folded it and dumped it on the grass in the shelter of the wall.

'Look, sit on that a minute, Miss, till we've got the tent up.'

She and Penny hurried then to help the others.

Pamela turned on Trisha.

'We don't need your help. Get your own tent up.'

Penny intervened, shouting to make herself heard above the rain which was pounding on the half-taut canvas.

'Let's just get one tent up, then we can get Miss Mooney inside.'

Pamela's eyes rolled skywards.

'Why did we have to be lumbered with her of all the staff?' she yelled.

Trisha snatched the guy rope that Pamela was holding and jerked it over the peg she had hammered into the ground. Then she straightened up.

'Listen, Cartwright, you stupid cow. You may know everything about slugs and everything about horses, but you don't know a blind thing about your own sex. If you can't see what's wrong with Mooney, you need a head operation. Now let's get this tent finished.'

Five minutes later, they helped an unprotesting Miss Mooney into the tent and made her comfortable on the groundsheet, with a rolled up sleeping bag under her head. A quieter Pamela had dug out some aspirins and in a little while, while the four girls huddled together in the other half of the tent, the teacher was asleep.

'Maybe, when the rain eases off we can get the other tent up,' said Pamela.

Penny shrugged. 'I can't see this letting up before it's dark. We'll just have to pack in together, I think.'

'What a life,' said Susi. 'Still, it'll keep us warm.'

There was silence for a moment, while Penny found chocolate in her rucksack and handed it round.

'Ha-hm?'

'What was that for?' asked Trisha staring at Pamela.

'What d'you mean?'

'I mean you did that without moving your lips.'

'Ha-hm.'

Susi pointed: 'That's outside the tent. Must be a cow.'

'Anybody in?' came a voice.

Trisha went on hands and knees to the laced up tent opening and peered out.

The large pink face of Ginger Joe, half hidden under the brim of an old trilby which cascaded water like a stream, was poised about a foot away from hers.

'Hey, you can't come in here, Joe. We've no vacancies.'

'No,' he yelled. 'Me mum says you must come inside the farm.'

'Can't do that.'

'Why not?'

'Expedition Camp, that's why.'

He shook his head as if she were mad.

'Well, in that case, you're going to need this.' From behind his back he held up a huge shovel.

'What for?'

'If you don't dig a channel at the top end you're going to be flooded out.'

# Chapter 35

Baxter looked round the crowded mess room with its haze of wet clothes and wet campers and muttered, 'Just what we needed. Duane missing again.'

'He can't have gone too far, if Clare's with him. She's very sensible.' Mrs Thomas called from across the room where she was helping the First Years to sort out their gear.

Baxter pushed his way over to them and confronted Christopher Stewart.

'Right, Stewart. Where did they go?'

Christopher bit his lip and looked down. Baxter took a deep breath.

'Now, come on lad, just for once forget the old Mafiosa Code, or the Old School Tie, or the Comrade's Oath or whatever, and just tell me where they went.'

'They went to the airfield,' squeaked Anita.

'Thank you. At least someone has something working between their ears. And what were they after at the airfield – collecting Spitfire numbers?'

'Looking for the ghost,' added Anita.

'Oh lord,' said Baxter. He turned to Miss Peterson who had pushed her way over from the outside door.

'Listen, Maureen,' he said, very quietly. 'This is a bit more than a lark, I'm afraid. If there is someone hanging about on that airfield, maybe some nut or other, as PC Hodges was hinting, then those kids could be in danger.

Her eyes widened.

'You could be right, Geoff. We'd better get over there.'

'Look, we don't want a general panic. You, Roy and I can go, but discreetly. I'll give the nod to Dan to watch things.'

He signalled to Hopwood and Roy Wilmot and the four of them struggled across to the doorway. Outside, the rain was still sheeting down. But the thunder had died away to a low grumble over the other side of the forest. Only an occasional flicker of lightning outlined the grey skyline.

Baxter turned in towards the other three.

'We're going over to the airfield to look for Clare and Duane. Can you look after things here, Dan?'

'Sir!' Anita's voice across the room was excited.

'Just a minute, Anita,' answered Hopwood, across his shoulder. 'That's OK, Geoff. I hope things are going to be all right.'

'Sir!'

'Oh, what is it, Anita?' Hopwood said impatiently.

'It's Duane, sir. He's behind you.'

Baxter and Hopwood swung round. Standing in the doorway, soaking wet, were Duane and Clare.

'Where have you two been? You've . . .'

'Sir, sorry sir.' the words tumbled from Duane's lips. 'It's all right sir. We've found the ghost sir, and he wants . . .'

'He what?'

'I'm afraid it's all my fault,' said a tired, old voice from the doorway. The campers standing nearest the door gasped as they saw the thin figure with the wounded face, the rain-soaked, patched and threadbare blue-grey serge of the uniform.

'Good grief,' muttered Baxter. 'John Mills, or is it Leslie Howard?'

# Chapter 36

Pamela Cartwright clambered to her feet in the cramped little tent and pushed to Trisha's side.

'Look Trisha, I'll do the ditch digging. You lot can fix the sleeping bags and make some grub.'

'I can dig, you know,' retorted Trisha.

'I didn't mean that, stroppy,' answered Pamela. 'I just happen to know how it's done. You turn a turf and make a shallow channel all round the top of the tent to lead off the water. Where the rain strikes that bare patch under the wall it'll come off in a flood before long. I should have thought of it first.'

She grinned at Trisha.

'Look, I agree, I don't understand human beings, but horses and shovels I am good at.'

She climbed through the narrow gap at the tent opening and took the shovel from Ginger Joe.

'You'd better get back and watch Emmerdale Farm or whatever Joe, you'll catch your death out here. Honest, we'll be all right. Only we can't go back and face the rest of 'em and tell them we spent the night in your barn.'

'Our mum was going to give you the spare room,' said Joe, shaking water from his hat and clamping it down on his head again. 'Still, please yourselves, catch pneumonia if you want to.'

He poked his head through the gap again.

'See you before you go, Trish?'

'If you're very good,' she told him. 'Now vanish if you don't mind. You may not know it but you're looking into a ladies' bedroom.'

He disappeared and the three girls set about fixing the inside of the tent while Pamela laboured with her shovel outside.

Half an hour later, the four of them were crammed together inside the tent again, struggling to open tins to make a cold meal.

'At least we'll be warm tonight,' said Pamela, 'like bugs in a rug.'

'You should know,' said Trisha.

'Do give over, you two,' said Susi.

'It's all right,' answered Pamela, 'there's no harm in the girl.'

Trisha was about to give a smart answer when they heard a cough outside the tent opening. Penny, who was nearest, leaned over and unlaced part of the canvas. Ginger Joe's pink face and ginger curls appeared in the opening.

'Mum says if you don't want the spare room, you've got to have this.'

He pulled his head back from the opening. A second or two later, a large saucepan was pushed through the gap by the tent pole.

'Careful with that. It's hot. It's rabbit stew.'

Followed by another metal dish.

'And that's plum pudding – home made.'

But Joe hadn't finished yet.

The canvas was pushed back and a large enamel teapot came through, followed by a tall blue milk jug and five china cups.

'Gosh thanks,' said Penny. Impulsively she kissed him. His face vanished instantly.

'Hey, Lewis, just watch it,' said Trisha.

'Never mind about that,' said Susi. 'Let's get fed.'

# Chapter 37

Loaded with sleeping bags and other gear, the campers poured through the Nissen hut door and gazed in amazement at the inside of the hut with its neat double line of beds.

From the stove in the middle of the room radiated a haze of heat. From a roof girder hung a tilley lamp which cast a wide arc of light across the concrete floor. Overcoming their surprise on the instant, the Grange Hillites charged across the floor, ignoring Baxter's shouts for order, and distributed themselves over the beds.

'It's all right, I have enough beds in the end rooms for the teachers.' The airman stood behind him, his ravaged face lit with a faint smile.

'I haven't been so near so many people for thirty-five years,' he said quietly.

He sat down on a nearby bed and slowly, curiously, the campers gathered round him. Some of the younger ones gazed at him boldly, inquisitively, others averted their eyes from his face. He looked round at them.

'It's not pleasant, is it? People don't like looking at my face, and I don't blame them. I feel more comfortable living on my own. I always have done since ...'

'But, sir, why?' Duane spoke encouragingly, as if he felt the need to help the airman explain himself.

'The world thinks I'm mad. They're right, in a way. They did try to certify me once. Then they tried to put me inside for trespassing on Ministry of Defence property. But I just moved on, from one place to another.'

'This isn't your ...'

'No. My old airfield's reserved for missiles now. The next time they scramble from there will be the last, for all of us. War was always mad, but now it has no meaning at all.'

'But, if . . .' Duane was baffled, 'why do . . . ?'

'It is something almost impossible to explain to anyone who has not shared danger with close comrades. Breakfast in peace and quiet together, death in the afternoon, and a pint and a song in the evening again. Those who share such things are like no other people you ever meet. Most men never find such friends again. I am different from others. I have never looked for them.'

He rose from the bed and walked down the hut to the room beyond, returning with a large black kettle. Taking an iron bar he lifted the top from the stove and placed the kettle on the open mouth.

'Water from the rain but, fruit and vegetables from the ground – shelter courtesy the Ministry of Defence . . . I'm still on the unit strength.'

He looked round at the bewildered faces.

'Every now and then I put on my civilian suit and hitch a lift into Bexford for my pension.' He grinned. 'The trousers got so threadbare, my pants showed through and I had to walk in sideways for fear of giving offence. Now they don't take any notice. I'm a tramp, I smell a bit, I'm mad, but they know I was useful once . . .'

Pogo's question burst out.

'Sir, your . . .'

'Sh!' said Clare, but the airman waved his hand.

'My face? It doesn't matter now. Our plane crashed, in flames. Crew of three. Our pilot dragged me clear and left me half dead on the ground while he went back for our oppo. The plane blew up and for months afterwards I knew nothing – until they put my body back together again, and as much of my mind as they could.'

He looked around him again.

'You all think it was a great heroic time, and so it was. But it was also crazy. The good part was that we were together and we shared. Today, outside in the world, they do not share any more. They fight, but each for himself. And no one wins.'

His eye caught Christopher Stewart's.

'You, young man, want to argue with me. I have not had an argument for many a year. But maybe later. The kettle's boiling now. Let's eat.'

He walked back to his room and returned with an old, blackened enamel teapot. Plucking up the kettle from the stove, he sent a stream of boiling water into the pot. He looked round again at the silent campers.

'When you people were singing last night, I crept up to the wire and watched you – all together – just as we used to be, all friends, sharing the whole life, eating, sleeping, working, playing together. You have something there. Don't let anybody spoil it for you.'

He grinned his twisted grin. 'End of sermon.'

Benny raised his hand.

'Sir. Was it you who put all those notices on the oak tree?'

'Notices? No, son, just one, about the latrines, I couldn't let that go by, could I?

'Who's ready for tea?' he asked.

# Chapter 38

At the crack of dawn the expedition campers came to life and disentangled their bodies from each other.

Groaning, Pamela Cartwright struggled across Penny's body and peered out of the tent opening.

'Hey, everybody. Rain's stopped, blue skies, sunshine. It's going to be a great day.' She turned round.

'How are you, Miss Mooney?'

Miss Mooney stirred and opened her eyes.

'Oh, I feel as though I've slept for days.' She looked round at them. 'I made a cosmic mess of things, didn't I?'

'Don't be silly, Miss Mooney,' said Penny. 'If you'd been feeling OK, you'd have coped. As far as we're concerned, and,' she paused, 'as far as the rest of the camp *and* the camp log is concerned, it's been a complete success.'

'Yeah,' said Trisha, 'and Ginger Joe will keep his mouth shut or else.'

'Well then,' said Miss Mooney, sitting up in her sleeping bag, 'I suggest we get ourselves ready, strike camp and make our way down to base.'

'But isn't Mr Hopwood picking us up at 10 o'clock?' asked Susi.

Miss Mooney shook her head. 'I think that Mr Hopwood and everyone else have probably had their work cut out coping with the storm down there. In fact, that's one reason why I'm keen to get back. I think they'll need us to give a hand.'

She picked up her anorak and felt in the pocket.

'It's a bit squashed,' she said, pulling out a bar of chocolate, 'but it should make one strip a piece.'

Leaving the heavy gear at the farmhouse for the obliging Ginger Joe to bring down later, the five expo campers force marched down the hill and across the valley to the Fawley Grange camp site.

At eight-thirty am they came through the camp gate at the run.

'Hope they've made breakfast,' shouted Trisha.

'Anybody home?' yelled Pamela.

But there was no answer. The lines of tents were completely empty. The girls rushed from one to another peering in through the flaps. But there was no one there.

They hurried to the top of the field and pushed open the door of the mess room. But it was empty. Only the debris of yesterday's evacuation still lay on the floor.

Miss Mooney stared round in bewilderment.

'What can have happened? Where have they gone?'

'Excuse me?'

'Ah!' They turned and gasped in chorus at the sight of the shabby blue-clad man at the door.

'If you ladies would like to follow me, breakfast is ready.'

'Oh, I could kiss you,' said Miss Mooney.

'Madame. No one has said that to me since VE-day,' came the answer.

# Chapter 39

Baxter banged on a mess room table and the lunch-time chat died away.

'Right. We've decided that the Treasure Hunt will go ahead as planned, despite yesterday's hurricane and earthquake.

'There are six objects, hidden in six prominent places all within the area of the valley upstream as far as the other side of the woods, downstream as far as the mill pool. On this side the boundary is the airfield fence. Whatever happened yesterday, you all still keep out of there. On the other side the boundary is the Fawley to Welthorpe Road.

'Cross the river only by the road bridge and for Pete's sake keep clear of the boggy ground near the water. We don't want to have to get the farmer with his tractor and cable to winch you out.

'The area's divided into five sections with a teacher covering each. If you are lost, or in difficulty, sing out loud and clear. Mr Wilmot will be roaming about filming.

'Work together – as big a group as you like – but never less than two. You have three hours. At four o'clock there will be three, repeat three, sharp blasts on my whistle and everyone makes their way back here. Got it?' He looked round the room.

'Right, on your way.'

The campers streamed out of the mess room. Outside the sky was blue, the air warm as though the storm had never been. Only the raindrops glinting on the long grass recalled the downpour.

Tucker grabbed Benny and Alan. 'Come on, we'll start over the stream up in the badlands.' Alan hestitated.

'Come on,' urged Benny, 'MacMahon's booked. Don't waste your time.'

Alan still hung back, but Susi was over by the barbecue pit, where Dukeson and Hargreaves were building up the fire ready for the supper grill. While Alan waited, Eddie Carver came over from his tent and walked away with Susi.

Tucker and Benny looked at Alan a second or two, then waving their hands dismissively, they turned down towards the gate and the road over the stream.

Trisha watched Susi go, then turned to the other girls.

'One down, three to go? What shall we do?' Penny said in a loud voice, which made several campers turn round curiously, 'Oh, I'm not feeling so good. I'm going back to my tent for a lie down.' She walked away while the others glanced at one another.

'That settles it then, Cartwright. We'll have to make a gruesome twosome,' said Trisha.

Pamela grinned, 'I can stand it if you can. Where do we start?'

'Oh, downstream, I suppose. Doesn't make much odds.'

As the campers dispersed, the First Years still hung on. Duane signalled them to join him at the back of the mess hut.

'Hey, what're you hanging about for?' said Pogo, 'They'll all have been found before we can get going.'

Duane shook his head and held up the list of clues.

'No sweat. It'll be a piece of cake.'

'Piece of cake?' said Christopher derisively. 'You talk like a Second World War film these days. The old man of the woods really got to you, didn't he?'

'What's wrong with that?' demanded Clare, 'I thought he was great.'

'Who's got the list of clues?' said Duane.

Precious held up a piece of paper. Duane dug into his jeans pocket and produced another, larger sheet.

He spread it out on the wall of the hut. The others crowded round. 'Hey, that's a map of the whole area – hand-drawn –' said Christopher. 'It's a lovely job.'

'Course,' said Duane. 'He was a navigator, wasn't he? It's

got every important bit marked on it. Now read me off the first clue.'

Precious held up her list: 'Where the deadly beetle did its work.'

'Right,' answered Duane, running his finger over the map. 'Here we are, top of the slope above the mill pool. Lone dead elm. Pound to a penny that's it. 'He looked round at them. 'So we go straight there and have a look, no time wasted.'

'No,' said Christopher. 'Let's got through the list of clues first and work out a route, to save time.'

'Great,' said Anita, 'save my feet as well.'

# Chapter 40

The scrublands high above the stream were rough and stony and the bushes still steamed in the afternoon sun. Insects drawn out by the sun hung in clouds. Tucker and Benny made their way slowly, slapping arms and faces and puffing gently.

'Hey,' said Benny, 'what clue are we following?'

'Clue?' Tucker stared. 'I'm not following a clue. I'm looking for the quarry.'

'Quarry? What for?' demanded Benny.

'Ginger Joe's mate Barry told me the other night. He reckons it's great – still some tunnels in the side of a cliff.'

'Could be a bit risky,' ventured Benny.

'Come on, it's a lot better than poking around in wet bushes looking for stupid clues.'

Benny shrugged and followed.

They climbed on. The ground had begun to slope less steeply as they came to the far side of the valley.

'Alan never came, did he?'

'No, d'you reckon he's following Susi?'

Tucker shook his head and paused for breath. The bushes were opening out in front of them and the breeze was cooler.

'I don't think he's bothered about her. I think he wants a tumble with Carver.'

'He's crazy. Carver'll break his arm for him.'

'Alan's pretty good. And he's mad, too.'

'Carver's better and he's iron. He could be deadly.'

'Well, that's Alan's look out. If he wants to get his head kicked in, it's his head.'

Tucker charged on with Benny on his heels, and they burst through the bush screen on to open ground.

A few steps further and Tucker jerked violently backwards throwing Benny to the ground.

'What are you doing, bird-brain?' he yelled.

'Saving your life.' Tucker pointed. Two yards in front of them, the ground gave way into open air. 'We've found the quarry, all right,' he said, breathlessly.

Benny crawled on hands and knees to the edge. Beneath him the raw brown surface of the quarry wall, fissured and ridged, dotted with clumps of weeds clinging to its face, dropped sheer away. The ground below seemed a long way off. Tucker joined him. 'That's useless,' he muttered.

'What is?'

'Well, we've come the wrong way round. It'll take hours to get round.' He pointed. 'Look, the tunnels are way over the other side.' He collapsed on to his stomach. 'Hey, it's hot up here. We could sunbathe.'

Benny grabbed Tucker's arm. 'Hey, look!'

'Don't want to. Where?'

'On that ledge – there, about half way down.'

'Where? Oh there. S'only a bird.'

Benny looked down again. Some twenty feet below them on a broad ledge that ran for several yards on either side, a small creature was huddled, its wings fluttering frantically. In the air some ten feet out, a parent bird hovered.

'It's hurt,' said Benny. He searched the quarry face. 'Hey, we can get down.'

'No way!'

'We can. There are good footholds. We can't leave the thing there.' To Tucker's amazement, Benny swung himself over the grassy lip of the cliff and, hanging on for a second or two, slid out of sight. Taking a deep breath, Tucker followed. It was easier going than he'd expected, though some of the footholds where the lighter Benny had stepped crumbled a bit under Tucker's weight.

'I'm there,' Benny called up to him. Tucker looked down. His head swam. He thought he'd die there and then. He turned his face to the quarry side, and slid down slowly, holding on to every crack and jutting stone. His foot below him missed its hold and went into space. He pressed his body desperately against the quarry face. He was sliding

123

down. A shower of earth and small stones hit him, filling hair, eyes and mouth. He was going.

'Be-e-nn-y-y.'

He hit the ledge with a thump, his knees jamming into the cliff face. Benny had seized him round the middle and the two of them clung to one another while earth, sand, stones and clods of grass cascaded round them and thumped down to the ground below. Tucker looked down, then back again quickly.

'Sit down,' yelled Benny, urgently. Tucker squatted. The ledge was firm rock. He was safe. He looked up cautiously. For ten feet above them, toeholds and hand-holds had vanished – the quarry surface was blank, still trickling with dislodged soil.

'We're stuck,' he said to Benny.

'Genius,' answered Benny. 'Look there.' He pointed, and Tucker followed the direction of his arm. On another ledge several feet to their right, sat the 'injured' bird, still fluttering its wings. But now the parent bird perched by its side feeding it.

'That's the last time I'll do a good deed,' he told Tucker.

Tucker looked at him, then pointed below them.

'You could be right. It's about two miles down.'

# Chapter 41

When the campers had left, Penny made her way back to her tent. The others had accepted her story of not feeling well without any question. That was how she wanted it, for she had a plan in mind.

Inside her tent, she got out writing pad and pen and carefully wrote out a notice, imitating as far as she could the shaky characters used by the Scribbler. She wrote:

HIS FATHER MAY BE A VIP, BUT HE'S A RAT. IF SOMEONE FINDS HIS PHOTO COLLECTION IT COULD BE ALL UP WITH HIM.

Then she left the tent, walked carefully to the old oak tree in the middle of the meadow and fixed the notice to the trunk. Further up the field Dukeson and Gary Hargreaves were busy with the barbecue pit. Smoke was rising and she could hear music playing. They had a trannie going and were taking no notice of anyone else.

Penny stole back to her tent and waited. She stuffed a rolled up shirt into the division at the back of the tent to make herself a spy hole, then she settled down to watch, making herself comfortable. The air in the tent was hot, but she did not dare have the flaps up. She waited, yawning. Her head dropped. She jerked up. Mustn't go to sleep.

Easier said than done. Her head dropped again. She stood up, stretched her legs, touched her toes and dropped down on her knees again, eye fixed on the gap in the canvas and the view it gave her of the field and the old oak. Minutes passed and she dozed off.

The tent canvas shook. She was awake. Someone had tripped on a guy rope in passing. The person swore and she recognized the voice, quiet as it was. Coming closer to her spy hole she saw a figure moving away towards the tree. There was no doubt who it was.

At the oak tree, the figure stopped, attention caught by

the notice. There was a moment's pause, then a hand reached out and tore the paper down. Penny got to her feet, then dropped down again. Mustn't spoil it all by rushing. She stared as the figure turned aside and bent down at the foot of the tree, searching for something. A moment later it got up again, turned, and went hurrying back to the lines to vanish into the tent opposite Penny's.

She waited. The tent flap opened. Someone hurried past her tent again, missing the guy ropes this time, and was gone. Penny hesitated a few seconds, then peered outside. The lines were empty. Ducking low she hurried across the empty space and into the tent opposite. She wasted no time, but pulled out rucksacks, spread out clothes, poked around until she found what she wanted. A large flat cigarette box, inside a plastic carrier bag.

She opened it and some twenty prints spilled out on to the groundsheet, together with film rolls. Gathering them together she paused a moment, listening. No one was near, it seemed. She began to study the prints. Some were clear, some were muzzy. Many had been taken in poor light. But faces were recognizable. Some were trivial – the face of a first year, sneaked fag in mouth; a third year with a crafty bottle outside the White Hart. Others were vague but more unpleasantly suggestive – was that Mrs Thomas and Roy Wilmot? Baxter and Miss Peterson. Ah, there were Tucker and his mates and the law from Fawley ...

She crammed all the pictures back into the box and put back the clothes and other belongings.

She took the pictures and films and put them in their box. The carrier bag went back into the rucksack. Clothes and all were replaced. Quietly she got up and left the tent. She'd take all these prints and films up to the mess room, look them over again and decide what to do.

Two yards from the tent she heard a noise and looked up.

'Caught you, Lewis. Thought you'd do that. Now give me that stuff.'

Doyle stood in front of her, blocking the way.

# Chapter 42

Susi and Eddie Carver had gone only a little way into the woods when Alan Humphreys confronted them from the other side of a small clearing. They moved to go past him. He shifted his ground. He ignored Susi, he was looking at Carver.

'Oh come on Alan, there's no need . . .'

'I'm talking to him, not you,' Alan replied.

'Listen, mate, she don't want to talk to you and I don't want to talk to you, so get lost, will you?' Eddie Carver spoke pleasantly, but the look on his face was deadly.

Alan said, 'I don't think I want to talk to *you* really, Carver,' and he stepped forward a pace or two.

'Oh, like that?' answered Carver, pretending surprise.

Susi looked rapidly from one to the other. She suddenly felt anxious – for Alan – but furious with him at the same time.

'Don't be so childish, Alan. Can't somebody just be with somebody else without . . .'

She plucked at Eddie Carver's sleeve, and headed for another path leading out of the clearing.

At the word 'childish', Alan had stopped. He half turned, but he did not follow them. As they pushed on under the trees where the wood grew more thickly, Susi looked back. Alan was standing, looking after them. Again she felt angry, then a little afraid again.

'Come·on,' urged Carver.

'What's the hurry?' she asked, baffled by the tone of his voice.

He did not answer, but after a few minutes when Alan was well behind them and out of sight, he turned to her again.

'I'm glad you did that.'

'Did what?'

'Told him to get lost. Some blokes need to have it written out for them.'

'Have what? I don't get you Eddie.' Susi tripped on a grass tuft and he grasped her arm to steady her.

'Oh, don't be so dim,' he said roughly.

She stared at him. He still had her arm in his grip.

'Can we slow down a bit, Eddie?'

He slackened his pace, but held on to her.

'I was only trying to tell him I'm not reserved for anybody. I please myself who I go about with.'

'Oh, yeah. And right now, you're out with me, OK?'

'OK.' She said unsurely. 'Where shall we go Eddie?'

'Treasure hunting?' he grinned.

She smiled uneasily. The afternoon was turning a bit stupid on her. She felt angry and confused.

'Come on, there's a place up here I found the other day,' said Eddie. 'Little Humphreys won't find us, nobody'll find us.'

'What place?'

'Old cottage. Bit of a ruin, really, but one room's dry inside. Too much damp grass out here – catch your death or something.'

'Hey Eddie, I don't want to spend my afternoon in any rotting old cottage.'

'You'll like it when we get there.' He grinned again. 'Come on.'

'Eddie, you're hurting my arm.' Susi's voice was unsteady.

'Oh, come on.' He tightened his grip and walked on more quickly.

# Chapter 43

Baxter stood at the foot of the quarry and looked up at the ledge. Tucker and Benny looked down.

'Beam us down, Scotty,' whispered Tucker.

'Jenkins, you disgusting little Smurf,' roared Baxter, 'how did you get up there?' His eyes swept the face of the quarry cliff.

'We got down here, sir,' said Benny.

'Down?' yelled Baxter. 'You couldn't have got down. There's no *way* down.'

'There *was* sir,' put in Tucker. 'But it sort of vanished.'

'I'll vanish you when ...' Baxter stopped. Then, 'What were you doing?'

'Rescuing an injured bird.'

'Well where's the bird now, then?' demanded Baxter suspiciously.

There was a silence, then Benny said in a small voice.

'It flew on to another ledge.'

'It flew?' Baxter breathed in twice. 'When I get you down here, you are *never* going to fly to any other ledge again, lad.'

He surveyed the quarry face for the second time. 'Well, now, let's see. It's about twelve or fifteen feet up.'

'No sir, nearer fifty,' said Tucker.

Baxter glared at him. 'I wish you *were* Jenkins; then I could bounce you off every inch of it. Now, there is a way down. There's a slanting crack in the face, just below where you are. You can reach it easily.'

Benny looked over the ledge and then drew his head back.

'I can't even see any crack, sir.'

'Oh, hang on, lad. You're useless. What are you?'

Baxter moved to the edge of the quarry face, and called up.

'I'm going to climb up to the ledge. When I give the word, you lower yourself over the side and I'll guide your feet on to the footholds. Right?'

'Right sir.' Tucker and Benny looked at one another. Below them they heard scraping and puffing sounds as Baxter began his climb. There was a sudden muttered oath and a splattering sound as loose sand and stones tumbled down to the bottom. Then more heavy breathing, another choice word or two, and Baxter's hairy forearms and glowering face rose above the edge of their perch.

'Now, let's be having the first one. Gently does it. You Green, I think, you've probably got more sense. No! What the ...' Baxter's face suddenly vanished and from below came a rushing rattling sound as if the ground were giving way.

Tucker and Benny leaned forward as one, and grabbed at Baxter's wrists, as his fingers struggled to keep their hold on the rock.

'Hang on sir. We'll hold you till you get your foothold again,' gasped Benny.

'Yeah. Hang on sir, we won't let you down,' shouted Tucker.

Lower down the scrublands, Roy Wilmot, cine-camera in hand, was filming the First Years as they charged towards him laughing and shouting. Duane, in the lead, was holding out a package.

'Object No 1, sir,' he called.

Behind him Clare waved another package.

'Object No 2.'

'The game's over,' shouted Christopher. 'We've got the lot.'

Roy Wilmot put down his camera. 'How did you manage that? You've scooped the pool.'

'Just natural talent, sir,' said Duane.

Roy stared. 'You must think I'm a fool, Duane. It's only three o'clock, you can't have found them all.'

Precious grinned at him. 'We found them all at two o'clock actually, but we didn't want to spoil the Treasure Hunt for other people.'

'Now look here, you lot. Don't give me that. How did you do it? You were listening in on the staff meeting, weren't you?'

'We never,' said Duane indignantly. He paused, then pulled out of his back pocket his map and spread it out for Roy to see. 'Flight Sergeant Harris gave it to us. It's got all the main features of the area.'

'That's cheating,' burst out Roy.

'Oh, no, sir,' put in Christopher, 'just initiative.'

Roy glowered at them, then grinned. 'OK. Anyway we'd better go and find Mr Baxter so he can give the signal to call off the hunt.'

'Hey, great,' said Anita, 'pork chops for supper.'

Duane grabbed at Roy's arm. 'Sir, listen.'

'Listen to what?'

'Somebody's shouting.'

Roy looked about him. 'That's true, Duane. And that sounds like Mr Baxter.'

'He's shouting for help,' said Clare, excitedly.

'Where's it coming from?'

'Difficult to tell,' answered Roy. 'The sound's echoing.'

Duane opened his map again. 'Look, sir. We're over here on this side of the river, in the scrubland.

'Yes, but where?'

Christopher leaned over Duane's arm. 'Look, sir, there's a quarry. Can't be more than a hundred yards away. That way up the valley.'

Wilmot and the first years set off at a run, Roy blowing short blasts on his whistle as he ran. As they turned the bend at the mouth of the quarry, the shouts were louder.

'Up there,' yelled Anita, pointing. 'Mr Baxter. Hey, Tucker and Benny have rescued him.'

'Hang on, sir,' shouted Pogo.

Roy stopped. 'Listen Duane. You know the quickest way

back to camp. Run back with Christopher and Precious and bring a groundsheet, the biggest you can find. Only run like fun.'

He swung round to the quarry face and instinctively the cine-camera arced up to pan the ledge where Tucker and Benny, red-faced and sweating, supported Mr Baxter.

Baxter looked round wildly. 'Roy,' he yelled. 'Do you have to do that?'

# Chapter 44

As they pushed through the bushes that surrounded the tumbledown cottage in the middle of the woods, Susi was twisting in Carver's grip.

'Let go, you –'

'Oh stop being a big kid,' he grunted, and pulled her up against him. He looked down at her and grinned 'What was it you told Humphreys? Don't be childish. Or d'you really want to go treasure hunting?'

'Come on, kid.' He eased his grip and put his arm round her shoulders. 'Didn't mean to hurt your arm. Just impatient, that's all.'

As his hold slackened, Susi jerked free, hooked her leg behind Carver's and heaved.

He sidestepped, kept his balance and tightened his grip.

'Very good, Susi. Just not good enough.'

She drew back her leg and drove the point of her toe into his shinbone. He showed his teeth in sudden pain. His free hand came round and her ear sang as his open palm cracked across her face.

'Little bitch.' He took a thick strand of her hair and jerked it till the tears sprang in her eyes.

'We can do it the easy way, or the hard way. Either way you're going to . . .' He yanked on her arm and ran her across the grass to the broken cottage door. She grabbed for the lintel. He brought his fist down on her fingers. She dug her heels into the soft ground and he gripped her round the waist and heaved her off the ground.

'You want to get really hurt?' he asked. His voice grew quieter as they struggled and Susi grew more scared.

The musty smell of the rotting cottage wall was strong in her nostrils as he dragged her over the broken floor.

'Now.' He drove her against the wall until the breath left

133

her body in a great rush and black spots danced in front of her eyes. She was going to pass out. Her body drooped. He slapped her face again.

Suddenly he let her go. The cottage door flew back with a crash.

'Right, Carver, you bastard!'

Alan appeared in the doorway. Carver went for him in a huge lunge and the two crashed through the opening onto the open ground beyond. From the broken window Susi saw them roll out. Alan was up in a flash. For all his bulk, he could move. But Carver was up before him. He took Alan by the front of his shirt, slowly easily, and swung him over to roll against the cottage wall. Alan's head struck the brickwork. The sound sickened Susi. But Alan was up, coming in low, and he had Carver round the hips. That was his only hope, to get in close, where weight would tell. Carver's hands rose and fell and Alan was falling, down, down.

Susi forced herself to move. Drawing in huge, ragged breaths, she staggered across the floor and out of the cottage door. She reached the corner just as Alan was trying to rise from his knees, and Carver's booted foot was drawn back to go in and finish it. She looked round wildly, snatched up a brick that lay loose by the doorway. As Carver swung, she threw.

As Carver went down, she caught Alan's arm, dragged him up and the two of them ran into the trees.

# Chapter 45

'Hopeless,' said Trisha to Pamela. 'We've tried all the places that side.' They stood now on the road outside the camp gate.

'Do you reckon someone's been there first and cleaned out?'

Pamela made a face. 'Could be. Come on, let's try the woods on the other side.'

'Before I move another inch, I'm going back to my tent for a drink of something,' said Trisha.

'OK. We'll have five-minute break, then decide what to do next.'

'Ten-minute break,' said Trisha firmly, opening the gate and going into the field. Pamela followed her, shutting the gate slowly. Then she stopped and held up her hand.

'Who's that shouting?'

'Where?'

'Over by the tents.'

'Hey,' said Trisha. 'It's Doyley!'

'But who's he after?'

The question was answered in a second as a figure raced from behind the line of tents into the open ground near the mess hut.

'Hey, it's Penny,' called Pamela. 'Doyle's chasing her.'

'That can't be right,' said Trisha.

'I'm not being funny. Sounds as if he'd like to kill her. Come on,' Pamela set off at a gallop and Trisha followed her. They shouted as they ran and Penny turned towards them. Doyle was almost on her as they came up. As he grabbed for her, Penny threw something. Pamela caught it, and as Doyle changed direction passed it to Trisha.

With the other three hard behind her, Trisha charged over the grass to the barbecue pit, where Dukeson and Gary

Hargreaves, sweating over the glowing mass of charcoal, looked up in astonishment as the shouting quartet came towards them.

Adroitly Trisha skipped over the pit, getting the two sixth formers between her and Doyle. He stopped in his tracks, breathing hard. Penny rushed past him and dodged behind Dukeson to stop by Trisha's side. Trisha passed her back the package she was holding.

'You give that back, Lewis,' snarled Doyle. 'Or ...'

'Hey,' said Dukeson, looking up. 'What's all the aggro? You lot are supposed to be on the Treasure Hunt.'

Gary Hargreaves grinned. 'They're rowing over the treasure. Tut tut. Such enthusiasm.'

'That's mine,' gasped Doyle. 'They're private pictures.' He began to moved round the barbecue pit. But before he had made the circuit, Penny held the package over the fire.

'You come any nearer and I'll burn them.'

'You can't do that, Lewis.' Doyle looked sick.

'Hey, Penny,' Dukeson put in. 'If those are his you can't burn 'em.'

'You ask him what's in this package,' replied Penny. The two sixth formers turned to Doyle. For a second he said nothing, then, 'they're private pictures. She stole 'em from my tent. She's been poking around here before. She's bent.'

'You're the one who's bent, Doyle,' answered Penny, furiously. She turned to the others. 'Since he won't tell you, I will. He's been taking pictures of people – only they didn't know what he was doing ...'

'Hey, that could be a giggle,' said Gary. Dukeson shook his head. 'That would depend, wouldn't it, who and what? He might have you there, eh?' Gary was silent.

Penny went on. 'There are staff here, as well. He's got pictures of everything that could stir up trouble when we get back.'

'OK,' said Dukeson. He looked at Doyle. 'Let's all go up to the messroom and have a look at them. If they're harmless, I'll guarantee Penny will give them back.'

'I won't' said Penny. 'Because they're not harmless and he knows it. He's the one who's been writing those notices.'

'I'm not,' shouted Doyle. 'It was that old bloke up on the airfield. He's bent, he's been spying on us all the time. He admitted it.'

'Oh, no, Michael Doyle,' said Penny. 'We all heard what he said. He wrote one and one only, the very first. You wrote the rest. You copied his writing, The pad's in your rucksack. That was why we never found that first notice after it was passed round at the camp meeting.'

'Come on then Doyle,' said Gary, 'if you're in the clear you can prove it by letting us see those pics.'

Doyle did not answer. Instead he turned and rushed across the grass.

'Hey,' said Pamela, 'he's going into our tent. Stop him.' But before they could move, Doyle appeared again, at the run, waving a large folder in his hands.

'What's that he's got?' asked Dukeson.

'It's my camp log, that's what,' said Penny.

'That's right,' sneered Doyle, coming up to the opposite side of the fireplace and holding out the folder.

'Tell you what, Lewis. I'll swap you. My version of what's happened on the camp, for yours. Then we can see what the old folks at home think of both. You show 'em what they think goes on and I'll show 'em what really goes on.'

'You mean what goes on in your tiny mind, Doyle,' said Pamela. She made a lunge at Doyle to snatch the folder from him but he dodged clear and slipped to the end of the fire pit away from the rest of them.

'OK, Lewis,' he said. 'What's it going to be?' He opened the folder, took out the first sheet, cleared his throat and began to read, imitating her voice. 'Camp Log, Day One. ETD 0830 hours from Paddington Station – all nice boys and girls and their lovely teachers started off, good as gold on the lovely trip – at public expense.' He held the paper in the air and let it flutter down into the flames.

Penny bit her lip. 'You're a slug, Doyle. You don't give a damn for anyone or anything, unless you think there's something in it for you. You don't understand doing anything for anyone else, unless it's worth your while. You make me sick. If everyone at school were like you, what sort of a place would it be?'

Doyle smiled, 'So you think Grange Hill's such a marvellous place?'

'No, I don't. But a lot of people put in a lot of work – more than they get paid for – and I don't see why you should put your dirty little paws on it. You know parents get worried over what goes on at school and you just want to stir it up.' She paused, 'You're bent, hanging round the back of the latrines, hiding in the doorway at the White Hart, like a Peeping Tom.'

'You know your trouble, Lewis? You're just too good to live. But, it's all talk, isn't it, just talk ...'

Carelessly, he took another sheet from the folder.

Penny's eyes opened wider. She took a deep breath.

Then slowly, she opened Doyle's box and scattered the pictures and films up and down the glowing embers in the pit.

'You –' Doyle shrieked as the flames suddenly blazed up and his fortnight's work was reduced to ashes. Opening Penny's folder he shook it wildly just as Pamela reached his side and seized his arm. In another minute Penny's fortnight's work had flared into a blackened mass in the middle of the pit.

'Hey what's all this?'

Miss Peterson and Mrs Thomas, with some of the Second Years, came across the grass from behind the mess hut.

Penny faced her. 'I'm afraid, Miss Peterson, my camp log has just gone up in smoke.'

'Good Lord,' Miss Peterson looked at the circle round the fireplace. 'Who did that?'

'I'm afraid it was just one of those things. One led to another,' answered Penny. The others were silent.

'Well,' said Mrs Thomas, 'we shall all have to put our heads together over supper tonight and see what we can remember.'

'I'm hungry,' said one of the Second Years.

'Won't be long,' answered Dukeson. 'Supper's in just under an hour. That is if you'll all let us get on with it.'

As they turned to move away from the fireplace, they saw two groups arrive on the camp field from opposite directions.

First came Duane and his mates, all chattering like monkeys, and carrying with them a large groundsheet. Behind them came Mr Baxter, limping slightly, helped along by Roy Wilmot and Tucker. Benny, also limping, brought up the rear.

'Well, there must be quite a story there,' said Mrs Thomas. Miss Peterson grinned wryly.

'I think there will be more than one version, somehow.'

From the other side of the field came Eddie Carver, head bound up with a strip of what seemed to be shirt-sleeve, grubby and slightly bloodstained. He was helped along by Mr Hopwood.

'What on earth has happened to Eddie Carver?' said Roy Wilmot in amazement.

'He can't remember,' said Hopwood, 'but he thinks he fell and hit his head on a brick.'

'Ah,' said Baxter, limping up to the fireplace, and looking round at the crowd. 'It looks as though the Treasure Hunt has ended. The First Years have cleared the field. Any more casualties?'

'I don't think so,' answered Miss Peterson, who had been counting heads. 'But we still seem to be two missing.'

'Who's that?'

'Susi MacMahon and Alan Humphreys.'

'Ah, well I doubt if they've got up to any mischief,' leered Baxter. 'I suggest we all go and dress for dinner.'

139

# Chapter 46

Camp was over, and the Grange Hillites were ready to move off. The tents were struck, the site tidied up and the first party was climbing into the mini-bus to drive to Fawley Station.

At the last moment Miss Peterson, who was counting heads, turned to Mrs Thomas.

'Not again. Duane's missing.'

'Oh, Duane,' answered Mrs Thomas. 'He's OK. Clare and he are just saying goodbye to a friend.'

Miss Peterson grinned and turned to the campers.

'Right, you lot, get aboard.'

When the first party had driven off, Ginger Joe drove up with Lola in the cab of his old green truck. He jumped down and greeted Trisha. While the others laughed and joked round them he said, 'Hey, Trish. Will you drop us a line when you get back?'

She grinned, 'Might do. Trouble is nothing ever happens down our way. It's all going on, here.'

'Here? Never. Quiet little place, this.'

'Oh yeah? Anyway, I'll see. I'm not much good at letter writing.'

Ginger Joe turned to Tucker who stood chatting with Lola and Benny.

'Hey, Tucker. It's going to be half an hour till the mini-bus gets back. No point wasting time. Tell you what – I'll give you all a lift to the station.'

Tucker turned and looked Ginger Joe in the eye.

'Shall I tell you what you can do with your old truck, Joe?' he said.